I0754846

force of nature

force of nature

Melissa Clark

Farrar Straus Giroux
New York

Farrar Straus Giroux Books for Young Readers
An imprint of Macmillan Publishing Group, LLC
120 Broadway, New York, NY 10271 • fiercereads.com

EU representative: Macmillan Publishers Ireland Ltd, 1st Floor, The Liffey Trust Centre, 117–126 Sheriff Street Upper, Dublin 1, D01 YC43

Library of Congress Cataloging-in-Publication Data
Names: Clark, Melissa, 1970– author
Title: Force of nature / Melissa Clark.
Description: New York : Farrar Straus Giroux Books for Young Readers, 2026. | Audience: Ages 12–18 | Audience: Grades 10–12 | Summary: On her sixteenth birthday, Chloe Lovejoy learns she has inherited the role of Mother Nature from her grandmother and must secretly balance school, family, and first crushes while protecting the world and keeping her new powers out of the wrong hands.
Identifiers: LCCN 2025029494 | ISBN 9780374394356 hardcover
Subjects: CYAC: Ability—Fiction | Nature—Fiction | Weather—Fiction | High schools—Fiction | Schools—Fiction | LCGFT: Fantasy fiction | Novels
Classification: LCC PZ7.1.C576 Fo 2026
LC record available at https://lccn.loc.gov/2025029494

First edition, 2026
Book design by L. Whitt
Interior images used under license from Shutterstock
Printed in the United States of America

ISBN 978-0-374-39435-6
10 9 8 7 6 5 4 3 2 1

force of nature

Chapter One

"Mother!" I yell from the kitchen, where I'm making a sloppy set of pancakes.

No answer from upstairs.

"*Mo*ther!" I yell again.

Crickets.

I know she can hear me. The house isn't big enough for sound to travel anywhere but up. She's probably buried deep under her blankets, with a few throw pillows over her head, trying to drown out the sound of my voice. I've often wondered who is the mother and who is the teenager in our family. Isn't she supposed to be the one downstairs making breakfast, and me the one refusing to get up?

The batter hisses and bubbles, indicating that it's ready, but when I try to flip the pancake over, it dissolves into a gooey mess on the spatula.

My best friend, Shannon, calls the firstborn in a family "the first pancake." She's the third, but she says the first kid is basically an experiment for the parents. What does that say about me? The first and only, as messy as my failed breakfast.

"Mo*ther*!" I yell in frustration.

Last night: Mom's twenty-year high school reunion. She invited five friends over for a pre-party, and they giggled like teenagers as they pored through photo albums from the past, over glasses and glasses of wine.

"Mommy needs this night," she'd told me as she wobbled out the front door.

I hate when she calls herself Mommy. I'm sixteen, not six.

"I hope Mommy enjoys," I'd said with a tight smile before slamming the door.

I add a pat of butter to the sizzling pan and pour in a new dollop of batter, then watch it expand and solidify. When it starts bubbling, I wait an extra minute, and—at last—I have created the ideal pancake. Both sides are perfectly browned at the edges, so I slide it onto a plate, grab the syrup and a fork, and march out of the kitchen and into my grandmother's room, which is located toward the back of the house.

Grandma's lived with us since Grandpa died, when I was only three. She is a beautiful mystery to me. To this day, I can never fully digest the fact that she's my mom's mom. Grandma is so calm and nice and gentle—unlike Mom, who I'd describe as rough and prickly. I always find myself trying to envision their younger days, like Mom at my age starting to date, or Mom learning how to drive a car, Grandma white-knuckling it in the passenger seat while Mom slams on the brakes.

In her bedroom, as usual, Grandma has the Weather Channel on in the background. She's obsessed with the weather, and she talks to the TV like she's having actual conversations with the anchors. "Snow in the Rockies? You must be some sort of genius!"

Her favorite is the weatherman from our local news station, Duncan Sunshine. I can't tell if she loves him or hates him, but she's always watching him, and calling out when he gets something wrong. "A 3.8 earthquake in Southern California?" she says. "Try 4.2, Duncan Ding Dong!"

When Grandma notices me, her face softens into a warm smile.

"Pancakes? For me? But it's *your* birthday!"

Well, at least someone's acknowledged it. My sweet sixteen. And on the first day of school, no less.

So far, the only thing sweet about it is the maple syrup I've poured over this pancake. Grandma sits up and takes the tray, placing it on her lap. She's wearing her blue jumpsuit, like a onesie for old people. She wears it practically every day, with a different shirt underneath, and calls it her "uniform." Grandma spends most of her time behind the main house, in her office—which is really a converted garage next to the pool. She never lets us back there, but Mom says she's busy with art projects and puzzles and knitting and stuff. She shuffles daily from her bedroom to the office and back again, a well-worn path indicated by the dead grass.

"Happy birthday, darling," she says, placing a forkful of her pancake into my mouth.

I try to form the words "Thank you" around the fork.

"Where's your mother?" she asks.

"Sleeping."

"Still?"

"She's not feeling well."

"She's *hungover*," Grandma says.

A rush of something sweeps through me. Fear? Shame? Gratitude for someone actually telling it like it is?

"You're such a good girl," she says, reaching for my face. "I've got a surprise for you later today. A birthday surprise that's going to knock your socks off."

Oh my God. A car. It's got to be a car, right? I mean, I don't want to *assume*, but what else would really knock my socks off? Sure, I like jewelry, and books, and tech, but even though I don't have my license just yet, I *love* cars!

"I see your mind trying to work out what it is," she says. "Trust me, you'll never guess."

Ah, but I already have. Could it be one of those cute Mini Coopers? What color? Would she let me pick, or did she already choose it herself? I'd take any color except for that rusty one that looks kind of like puke.

"Mom and I will pick you up after school today, assuming she can pull herself together, God willing."

Yes! A public presentation of my new Mini Cooper! It'll be like this past spring when Brooklyn Weber's dad pulled up to school in a red Mercedes G500 with a huge white bow around it, gifting the car to his daughter on *her* sixteenth birthday.

"I can't seem to get out of bed today," Grandma says.

"So stay. You're allowed. An eighty-year-old lady like yourself."

Grandma shoots me a look.

"A seventy-two-year-old lady . . ."

Another look.

"A sixty-eight-year-old? . . . Ninety-year-old? . . . Seventy-nine-year-old?"

It's an age-old game between us. Grandma won't dish on her age, and Mom claims she doesn't know it, either. With her long, gray hair and her soft skin, Grandma could be anywhere between sixty-five and one hundred, for all I know. Sometimes when she twists her hair into a loose bun, she looks like a model, and I can picture what she might have looked like when she was my age. Would we have been friends? I bet we would have.

"Stay in bed, Grandma. However . . . young you are."

"Nah!" she says. "I've got things to do. Plus, what kind of grown woman stays in bed all day?"

We both know the answer to that.

I'm tapping my foot while sitting on the bench outside the guidance counselor's office, pretending to read the school's newspaper, *The Breeze*. Today is my first appointment with Mrs. Boyle, who lives her life to guide students over all sorts of hurdles, including college applications.

I'm a junior. I remember Dad dropping me off on the first day of ninth grade, not even sticking around to make sure I navigated the new campus okay. He beeped his horn from the second I exited the car until he was out of sight. He's still that embarrassing, and still thinks his car horn is a musical instrument.

I can hear engaged, enthusiastic talk coming from inside, and when the door finally swings open, I see Brooklyn Weber. "So, just to reiterate," Brooklyn says to Mrs. Boyle as she's gathering her backpack and papers. "In order of preference, it's Harvard, Yale, Stanford, Brown. And Princeton as my safety school."

Mrs. Boyle says, "You have a whole year to decide, Brooklyn. Who knows—your list might change."

"Doubt it," Brooklyn says. "My entire life has been in preparation for this." Then she looks over at me and says, "Oh, *you're* thinking of going to college?"

"Yes," I say, getting up from the bench. "And by the way, I don't think Princeton is anyone's safety school."

"Are you kidding me?" she says before walking away. "It's in *New Jersey*."

In my entire educational career with Brooklyn Weber—which has been since sixth grade, when she moved here from New York—I have never been fast enough to match her snide quips hurled in my direction. And there have been many, for reasons I'll never understand.

"Good morning, Chloe," Mrs. Boyle says, seemingly unaware of my exchange with Brooklyn. Or maybe she's just chosen to ignore it. She ushers me inside her office and thumbs through her file cabinet. There are flags and other paraphernalia of colleges and universities hanging on all four walls of the room: University of Michigan, MIT, Notre Dame, even Oxford. I wonder what flag I will contribute to the collection. "Junior year ready?" she asks. "Classes picked? ACT scheduled? Starting to think about far reaches and safety schools for college?"

Harvard, Yale, Stanford, Brown . . . definitely not the ones I'll be applying to.

"Welcome to the first of many meetings about your future!" she says.

"Yay," I say, trying to match her enthusiastic tone. The seat I'm in is still warm from Brooklyn's butt.

"Let's have a look at your transcripts." Mrs. Boyle reads: "B-minus, C, C-plus, B-minus, C-minus, C. Oh, here's an A-minus! . . . In Chorus," she says, her lips pursing together.

"I like singing," I confirm.

"Don't worry, Chloe," Mrs. Boyle says. "There are plenty of schools that overlook less-than-ideal grades. Let's get you focused on some extracurricular activities this semester. You know, I had a student a few years ago . . . almost all C's but a stellar record of community service. She studied hard for her ACT, wrote an excellent personal statement, and ended up at Smith."

I nod. Am I supposed to assume Smith is a good school? It sounds like someone's boring last name.

"You need to stand out from the pack," Mrs. Boyle says, raising her fist. "How motivated are you to do that?"

"I'm motivated," I say weakly.

"If you're motivated, this is going to be your year. Let me suggest you join a sports team this semester, and I'd like you to do something service-oriented on the side. You can volunteer at a day-care center, or a hospital, or walk dogs at the shelter, for example."

Babies, old ladies, and puppies flash before my eyes.

"And I highly recommend you get into an ACT study group," she says. "Especially if you're testing low."

Of course she assumes I am, and of course she's right. I blew through a practice test the other week at home and kind of bombed.

"It's going to be a busy year for you, Chloe," she says, bursting with enthusiasm. "But in all honesty, you're my favorite type of student. I love a good Cinderella story!"

"Cinderella story?" Shannon says. "Are your evil stepsisters making you scrub the floor again?"

"I *wish* I had sisters," I say.

We're sitting on the quad, post-lunch, pre–fifth period.

Felix rolls his eyes. "She means a rags-to-riches story," he says. "It's a classic fairy-tale motif."

"So, 'rags' being my C's," I say, "and 'riches' being some Ivy League college?"

"Exactly," Felix says.

"I think the whole meeting wouldn't have been so painful if I hadn't gone in *after* Brooklyn."

"Who cares about her," Shannon says.

"Why does she have to be such a snob?" I whine.

"Pretty and snobby," Felix says. "Some people are just born lucky."

"Mrs. Boyle wants me joining a sports team and volunteering at some old-age home. I mean, that's just so not me."

"You live with your grandmother," Shannon says. "Doesn't that count?"

"And can you imagine if I showed up at tryouts for the basketball team? They'd laugh me off the court."

"You're too little for basketball," Felix says. "What about gymnastics?"

"I get dizzy from somersaults."

Felix raises an eyebrow. "That's not normal."

"You don't *have* to do everything she suggests," Shannon says, lying back on the grass, angling her face toward the sun. "It's your life."

I shrug. "Yeah, I know." All of a sudden, I feel something tickling my cheek. I can't help it when I let out a shriek.

Felix jumps. "What?" he says.

"Calm down. It's a *fly*," Shannon says, swatting it away.

"I hate winged things," I tell them. Once, when I was little, I swallowed a fly on the inhale when I was laughing. I still remember the buzzing feeling at the back of my throat, and everyone cracking up as I tried, and failed, to spit it out. Don't even get me started on birds—though, thankfully, I've never accidentally swallowed one.

"I'm dreading my meeting," Felix says. "I only want to go to NYU, but I know Mrs. Boyle is going to make me apply to at least seven other places."

"How do you already know where you want to go?" I ask. The real question is: How come I have no idea?

"My parents went there. Plus, it's got one of the best architecture programs."

Well, that explains it. My dad dropped out of college. Mom did, too. While Brooklyn and Felix were busy plotting their college careers at the family dinner table, I was helping Mom upstairs after a few too many vodka cranberries.

"Close your eyes, Chlo," Shannon orders, sitting up suddenly.

"Is there another fly?"

"Stop. No fly," she says. "If you could get anything you wished for on your birthday, what would it be?"

I close my eyes, debating whether or not to tell them about my pending Mini Cooper. "Um," I say, then settle on, "Curtis Reed." The curly-haired cutie from Chorus who I've been crushing on for two years.

I hear the rustle of a backpack, then papers, the flick of a lighter, and the beginnings of the birthday song, which tells me that it's okay to open my eyes. I am presented with a red velvet cupcake with Curtis Reed's face outlined in frosting.

My friends start singing. *"Happy birthday to you, happy birthday to you! Happy birth—"*

"You guys!" I say.

"—day, dear Chloooooeeee. Happy birthday to you!"

"How'd you even do this?" I say, marveling at the black frosting as his curly hair.

"My sister's best friend works at a bakery," Shannon says, laughing.

"How'd you even get a picture of—"

"Yearbook!" Felix says. "Blow out the candle before you get wax all over his face. Unless you're into that sort of thing."

I wish for my Mini Cooper before blowing it out.

"Thanks, you guys!" I say, licking frosting off the candle.

"Since you're not having a party, we thought we'd bring the party to you," Shannon says.

It's true. Over the summer, Mom decided she couldn't—or wouldn't—afford a sweet sixteen for me, as so many of my friends had had. I'd cried for hours, wondering why she would deprive me of a birthday celebration, but now I think I know why.

The car. My Mini.

Felix says, "Maybe you can practice talking to Cupcake Curtis until you muster enough courage to speak to the real one."

Shannon nods in agreement.

"Shut up," I say. But they're right. My brain sputters like an old engine every time I'm near him, and instead of hitting the gas pedal, I always put the car in reverse. We often walk in to Chorus together, stand a few people away from each other, sing our hearts out, and exit together, all without saying a word.

"You guys, okay," I start. "I don't want to jinx it, but you have to come with me after last period to meet my mom and grandma in front of school."

Felix says, "Mom *and* Grandma? Something big, right?"

"I don't wanna say it out loud," I tell them, and instead mime my hands on a steering wheel and beep an imaginary horn.

Shannon shrieks in delight. "You're getting a car?"

"I don't know," I say. "But my grandmother hinted that this year's gift is really, really big."

"Is that why you didn't have a birthday party?" Felix asks.

"Probably," I say.

"Okay, I hope it's a car," Shannon says. "You know I hope it's a car. But you have to be prepared in case it's not. I'm only saying it to be a good friend."

"I know, I know. I am prepared," I lie, taking a giant bite out of Curtis's sugary head.

Shannon and Felix sit on the stairs nearby, doing homework, while I'm at the curb, craning my neck and waiting for my new car to arrive. Finally, around three fifteen, my mom pulls up in her old Chevy Blazer, Grandma in the back seat. Shannon spots them, too, and gives me a weak smile.

"Maybe they're driving you to pick it out," Felix calls.

My heart sinks as my mom rolls down the window and waves me over. It's such a normal gesture, which makes me think this gift will be more like a trip to the mall for a nice necklace—That's fine—a nice necklace is fine—but socks are not knocked off by that.

"See you tomorrow," Felix says.

"Call us with any news," Shannon says, holding up an imaginary phone.

I walk to the car, open the door, and settle into the front seat, turning to my grandmother in the back. It's rare that she ever goes out. She's not even in her uniform. Instead, she's dressed up in a flowing blue skirt and nice white blouse. Her hair is pulled back into a loose ponytail, and feathery earrings dangle from her ears.

"Hi, Grandma!" I say. "You look nice."

"For your birthday!" she says.

"No hello for your mother?" Mom says from the driver's seat.

"You're awake!" I respond, mock-surprised.

My grandmother kicks the back of my seat.

"Happy birthday," Mom says, an edge in her voice, as usual.

I realize we're not going to the car dealership, or even to the mall, as we approach the on-ramp of the freeway and head south. The radio is on, Frank Sinatra crooning about witchcraft, and the atmosphere is charged with a weird, unspoken energy, but nobody's revealing what's happening, so I sit patiently—waiting for the big surprise.

Around thirty minutes later, we exit the freeway and make our way west following signs to Parker Beach, and now I'm utterly perplexed. We are not beach people. I, especially, am not a beach person; I've always been irritated, even as a child, by the feeling of sand on skin, Mom chalking it up to some sort of "sensory disorder."

She parks in an empty lot and pops open the trunk, dragging herself out of the car and reaching in for something back there. What is it? What could it be?

She pulls out a picnic basket. I help Grandma out of the back seat. A picnic at the beach? That's my big surprise? The swell of disappointment must be visible on my face, because Grandma takes my hand and squeezes it. "Patience, sweetheart," she says.

We head to an old wooden table on the sand. The ocean is blue black—the beach practically empty except for a guy in the distance throwing a stick for his yellow lab. The waves are rough and loud. We all sit around the picnic table. Mom unpacks the basket: cheese and olives and hummus, some crackers and pita bread.

"Isn't this lovely?" Grandma says, lifting her chin to catch the scent of the salt air.

It's actually really chilly, but I nod and smile. Grandma's so dressed up it almost makes me sad.

"Mother, did you bring the—" my mom starts. "Never mind. Found them," she says, pulling out the plastic knives.

Not a set of car keys. Not a necklace. Quite frankly, I'm ready to get home, but I don't want to ruin the theatrics. I gaze around at the beach, thinking I should really be home studying for the ACT and figuring out some extracurricular activities. I shrink at the memory of Mrs. Boyle reading from my transcripts—*C-plus, B-minus, C-minus, C*—the sad letters rattling around in my head.

Mom gathers three red plastic cups and pours sparkling apple juice into all of them—yippee, fake champagne!—and raises hers for a toast. "Happy sweet sixteen to Chloe," she says flatly, and we clink cups.

I'm about to take a sip from mine, but Grandma presses my hand down. "Wait!" she says. "I have something I want to say.

"There's something I need to tell you," Grandma starts. "Something you need to know. I want you to listen first and then ask questions later."

I nod and glance at my mom, who is staring straight out toward the ocean. I follow her gaze but don't see anything specific—just water, just waves.

"Chloe, since the beginning of time, the Lovejoys have been a special group of women: My mother, Sylvia Tara. My grandmother, Ivy Tara. My great-grandmother, Myrtle Tara. And on and on throughout the ages."

Tara. It's my middle name, too: Chloe Tara Lovejoy.

"We've been bestowed with a power so great it's humbling," she says. "Our people can be traced way, way back in time. The Garden of Eden was named after Eden Lovejoy, who was rumored to have complete control over the elements, creating perfect conditions for Adam and Eve and, some say, the beginning of humanity as we know it."

I nod, pretending I'm following. Eden, as in the Garden of Eden, is my great-great-great-great-grandmother or something. Right. Got it. Mom's still staring, not even blinking. She has to blink at some point, doesn't she? The man and his dog have moved farther down the beach, near the volleyball courts, almost out of sight, but I can still hear the faint echo of barking.

Grandma reaches for something in her pocket. Her pale hand exposes an old-fashioned key—bigger than a normal key, though not by much. "It's for the Maparium," she says in a whisper, handing it to me. "The office."

I clarify, "The office in the backyard?"

She nods.

What she really means is: *The converted garage.*

I take the key from her. "Thank you?" I say. Because what else am I supposed to do? The key is heavy, ornate, a weight in my hand. Is this the big, giant birthday gift? Is this the sweet of my sixteen?

"What's in there is yours," she says. "It is unofficially yours starting today, and then *officially* becomes yours in five years, on your twenty-first birthday. You won't believe how fast time flies."

I picture piles of wool sweaters and paintings and drawings, a cruddy TV with rabbit-ear antennas. Or maybe she's a hoarder, like the ones I've seen on that TV show. Maybe there are a thousand cats in there, or at least a thousand dust bunnies. The door to the office is always locked, and I'm never allowed back there, so I really have no idea what to expect.

"With this key comes great responsibility," she says, cupping her hand over mine. "Some days you will feel burdened. But I trust you implicitly to carry on the responsibilities of our calling."

Oh no, is Grandma losing it? Is she suffering from dementia or something? Mom doesn't seem concerned. She sighs an *I'm so bored* sigh.

"Chloe Tara," Grandma says wistfully. "My beautiful little fertility goddess."

Fertility goddess? Me? The virgin? "Grandma . . ." I can't stand the confusion anymore. "What's going on?" Things are starting to feel dreamlike, and I'm wondering if I'll soon have the luxury of waking up.

"Mother," my mom finally says, irritated. "Just tell her straight out."

A wave crashes in the background. A seagull squawks.

"You're next in line to be Mother Nature, my dear," Grandma says to me in a hushed tone, a slow, broad smile forming across her crooked lips.

I'm staring at Grandma, her steel-blue eyes gazing back at me. Am I supposed to say something? Why would she say something so absurd as I'm next in line to be Mother Nature?

"Chloe, the key is for you, and you only," she instructs, glancing sideways toward Mom. I try to catch Mom's eye, too, but she won't meet my gaze.

I'm merely going through the motions when, instinctively, I make a fist and hold the key tight in my palm.

"There's going to be a learning curve, Chloe, but please don't worry. That's why this transfer of power won't be official for another five years. It was the same way for me when I inherited it over sixty-five years ago from my mother. Oh, it was a day I'll never forget."

I'm blinking furiously, hoping that this will wake me up. It's worked in the past, like this one time I dreamed I was falling down a well. I woke just before I hit bottom, my heart racing, but so relieved to be in my own bed.

"Listen carefully," Grandma gently says. "Once you're in the office, you'll find *The Book of Nature*. I don't expect you to read it all at once, but it will help get you started, and it should be your priority."

Listen, I repeat to myself, just in case this isn't a dream. So far, this is what I'm hearing: Grandma thinks she's Mother Nature, and so was her mother, and her mother, on and on down the line, and I'm somehow connected to the Garden of Eden. That's what I'm hearing, unless I've got some serious earwax buildup.

"But wait," I say, playing along with this story. "What about Mom? Shouldn't *she* be Mother Nature next if it's passed down through all the women?"

Mom seems angry that I even asked the question.

Grandma shakes her head no. "There's the way things *should* be, and the way things *are*. Do you understand?"

Nope, still don't.

"Chloe, the job is about maintaining balance, not necessarily harmony. It's math meets science."

C, C-minus.

"With a dose of psychology and art. It's going to look so overwhelming at first, Chloe," she says, sighing. "But you're a smart girl. A brilliant girl. You'll get the hang of it."

No one's ever called me brilliant before.

I mean, I don't believe it, of course. How could I? Why would I? But it seems like Grandma does. Like she's 100 percent convinced that she's Mother Nature.

I remember when Shannon's grandma got diagnosed with dementia last year and the doctors suggested they play along with whatever she said. Okay, I reason. I'll try that.

"You're M-mother Nature," I utter in a small voice. Even if she doesn't have dementia specifically, I decide right now to follow her down this strange yet compelling path to see where it leads.

She starts explaining about some electronic boards in the office and how they're set up and color-coded—that when things to the right are red, things to the left should be blue. Or is it green? What if things on the left are red? Grandma's talking, but her words are starting to blur, and soon I'm hearing: *Blah blah blah blah, something something, red, green, blue* . . . Only when she uses the word *empathy* do I pause and take notice, because it's on the vocabulary list for the ACT. *Empathy: noun, the ability to understand and share the feelings of another.*

"It's an enormous responsibility, but you will learn strength and power and empathy," she says. "It's a lot to follow, I know. But you're with me, yes, dear? I'm having trouble reading your expression. It will make more sense when we get home," she adds. "But I wanted us to be somewhere special today when I told you, so this moment would be seared in your mind forever. The sand, the sea, the sunset, and me—your old granny. I remember where I was when I was told I was inheriting the job of Mother Nature," she says wistfully. "We took a long hike up to the top of Morro Rock, back in the days when you were allowed up there, and I came down a changed person."

Mom is tearing into the pita, dunking it in the hummus before shoveling it into her mouth, like this is a normal picnic, a normal conversation. Why isn't she acknowledging that her mom is rapidly declining in front of our eyes?

"Eat, darling," my grandmother says to me. "Now, we enjoy the meal. Later at home, I'll show you the Maparium. We'll take a walk soon. It's going to be a spectacular sunset tonight—I can guarantee you that." She winks.

I smile too wide, my teeth clicking, pretending that this is normal, but all I can think about is what the hell I'm going to tell Felix and Shannon tomorrow at school.

Chapter Two

If you've ever had weirdness within your family, try driving home after learning your grandma thinks she's Mother Nature. Mom is complaining about all the slow drivers on the road, and Grandma's humming along with Frank Sinatra the entire ride, like it's just another normal day. I stare out the window, watching all the adorable Mini Coopers whiz past us.

Once we get back to the house, Mom busies herself unpacking the trunk while Grandma leads me through the backyard and unlocks the door to the office, because apparently there's more. I play along. "Darling, this is HQ," she says softly as I follow her inside.

In movies, the way they portray NASA headquarters—the beeps, the blips, the colorful blinking machinery, the hum of electronics, the banks of computer terminals—yeah . . . that's what it looks like in our garage. Our garage!

Grandma's "office" is wall-to-wall flat-screen TVs, from large to larger, and rows of twinkling equipment, like white and red and green Christmas lights. It's a recording studio—no!—an airplane cockpit—no!—it's SpaceX! The walls are covered in illuminated maps. The ceiling, the floor, everywhere! I'm afraid to step on anything. I'm afraid to make any sort of move. All this, here in our garage? This is no craft room. There are no knitting needles in sight, no wool sweaters pilling and piling in corners.

"What is going on in here?" I say, looking around at everything and processing nothing. Did Grandma go to the dollar store and buy all their maps? Where did she get all this tech equipment? This is so elaborate! Shannon's grandma just wore underwear over her pants. My grandma's condition seems a lot more advanced.

"You must be so tired," I say. "From the long day at the beach." I put my arm around her shoulder, ready to guide her back to her bedroom.

"What are you talking about, tired?" she says, shaking me off. "I'm not tired. I'm *thrilled* showing you your new world!"

"Okay," I say, resigned, wondering if Mom realizes the depth of the dementia.

"There's more," Grandma says, pressing a button.

Oh gosh, now what? What could this button near a doorway possibly do?

But it's not a doorway. It's an elevator, which I only realize when it opens. "Come, come," she says, leading me inside. I'm sure she sees my hesitation when she reaches for my hand and pulls me in. The elevator doors shut to reveal more maps.

We ride down, down, but where are we going? I feel like I'm at the Haunted Mansion ride at Disneyland.

My breathing is rapid and shallow. When the doors open again, we step out and into what I can only describe as a large cave, with a hologram of Earth spinning right in front of us. It is bigger, more spacious than the office above. It's the coolest thing I've ever seen in my life. Cooler than the dancing ghosts in the Haunted Mansion.

My head tilts skyward. Images rotate around the ceiling—of landscapes in Africa, the Grand Canyon, a volcano somewhere.

"Satellites changed everything," Grandma says. "And now drones. The images are as high-resolution as you can get." My mouth is as dry as the deserts projected on the walls.

There are also shelves, filled with books, but one book stands out: It's an antique, with gold-rimmed pages, and it's lit up in a glass case. It's as thick as a Bible, bigger than my chemistry textbook.

Grandma unlocks the glass case and reaches for it. "Here. This is *The Book of Nature,*" she says. I'm afraid to touch it, and she's struggling with its weight.

"Don't hurt yourself," I say. "I can see from here."

"Open it, dear," she demands, handing it to me.

I carefully turn its fragile pages to the first chapter.

"Why don't you read it out loud?" she suggests.

I hate reading out loud. I'm always worried about

mispronouncing words and stuttering. But Grandma is waiting, and so I do.

Making the Transition

The light has dimmed, and the past is the past. Forget all you know to be true, and greet the new world with an open heart. Welcome, Mother Nature, to a universe under your rule. Your twenty-first year is upon you, and the world beckons to your every whim. Your standards mark a global shift, and your lineage has prepared you well for the task.

The emotional transition on which you're about to embark is as unique as your fingerprint. The focus of this chapter will be on the physical demands of the job of Mother Nature.

First, it is imperative that you are well rested, as a clear mind is demanded of you at all times. Proper diet and nutrition are also required to sustain your energy level throughout the day. Becoming Mother Nature requires your undivided attention. Your focus will determine the success of your transition.

Mistakes are inevitable, but your ability to correct them will define your ultimate character. And it is your character that will define the world.

"Beautiful," Grandma says. "We'll do some readings like that every day."

"Every day?"

What is this book? And who wrote those words in striking calligraphy? Maybe this is what Grandma's been doing with her time back here, practicing her best penmanship and binding it together like some wacky art project. I look around for pens but don't see any. "Every day?" I say again.

She nods.

"But I'm not twenty-one," I say, still playing along.

"Right. Twenty-one is when we *officially* make the transition. But we have five years to ensure the smoothest transition possible. We have five years to train. Together."

I half expect the cave walls to collapse around us, and a laugh track to emerge, like I've seen on those TV shows. *Ha ha ha, had ya fooled! What? You really thought you were becoming Mother Nature?*

"Look over here," she says, guiding me to one of the maps against a far wall. "Only look. Don't touch." The map reveals rivers across the world, carved to make them look textured. There's so much to see, but I can't seem to focus on any of it. There is a bank of levers to the right of her, and a wheely chair. She sits and rolls over, setting her finger on one of the levers. "Look here," she says as she slides it up. "The rain. Listen."

"What?"

The *rain*? It's not raining outside! Or is it? We're so far down that it's hard to tell, but I do hear something.

"Come," she says, taking my pointer finger, placing it gently on the lever, and sliding it even farther up.

I take in a slow, cautious breath and release it in a puff.

"This quadrant is for California, and up here is Montana, and these levers control the East Coast, but over there we have South America, Panama, Colombia . . ."

"So you just move a lever, and it rains?" I don't know how she's pulling this off. Maybe she's a magician, or an illusionist, as they like to be called these days. Whatever she's doing, it's elaborate and incomprehensible. The best trick I've ever seen.

"It's a somewhat new technology. Well, new for me—within the past twenty years."

She stands and walks me back over to the illuminated glass case.

"*The Book of Nature* has everything you need," she says, replacing it and locking it back up. "And we'll have years to study it together. I know you'll have many questions. Wade can help you, too."

Oh no, a new character in this creative game. I feel I need to ask: "Who's Wade?"

"He's off-site, but you can always access him." She points to a black intercom sitting on a shelf above *The Book of Nature*.

"I've got to warn you, though," Grandma says, her tone growing serious, "while this work is glorious, it can sometimes be heartbreaking."

She tells me the floods, the volcanoes, tsunamis, windstorms, fires, they're all part of the gig. Mother Nature isn't necessarily responsible for all of these tragedies, but I'll have to be vigilant in monitoring them all. She tells me nature generally runs its course smoothly, and when it doesn't, there's a good reason. It's *people* who get in the way of all these natural processes when things go haywire. If only the *people* could do the right thing . . .

I just keep nodding like one of those bobblehead dolls.

I am not, she tells me, to blame for people's *actions*, because

I can't control people—no one can—but I am to focus on the shifts and demands of the earth. Earthquakes will be needed for lakes and mountains to expand, and volcanoes will erupt from built-up pressure underneath. Tornadoes will twist, distributing moisture where it's needed. The desert will bloom under torrential downpours.

I'm waiting for Grandma to snap out of whatever fever dream this is and dangle a Mini Cooper key fob in front of me. I search deep into her blue eyes, desperate for answers.

"You're Mother Nature now," she says as she directs me to the controls for wind, sleet, clouds, and snow, my breath quickening, my heart glugging. "The earth can be very demanding," she warns. "You'll understand. You'll learn to meet its needs."

She tells me about swiping a rainbow arc, triggering a volcano, a landslide, a tsunami, the northern lights. I'm in disbelief, taking in nothing. Blinking, blinking, blinking, like that cartoon character from the old days with the long eyelashes.

"The world faces insurmountable challenges—dying ecosystems, shrinking rainforests, species extinction, melting ice caps, and pollution," she says. "It used to be, back in the early 1800s, that my Great-Great-Great-Grandmother Flora could wash away the various pollutants with rain, but in the late 1800s, industrial pollution began in earnest, and now even the *rain* is polluted.

"*People*," she adds in a huff. "If only *people* could do the right thing and not pollute in the first place. Everything ends up in the water, but for some reason, I think that fact is almost too obvious for folks to comprehend."

I never, ever knew how passionate she was about environmental issues. Maybe a part of her brain got activated with this disease, and the environmental part just lit up like a Christmas tree. "Grandma?" I ask in a small voice that surprises me.

"Yes, dear?"

"This is for me?" I say, pointing to everything. "Are you sure you want me to have it?"

"It's your birthright," she says.

"But—not Mom's?"

"How could I?" she says. "You understand."

"Doesn't she—"

Grandma puts her crooked finger over my lips to shush me. "Don't be so worried. I'm allowed to skip a generation if that's what I want to do. And it is. *You're* the one I trust."

Eventually, she says she's exhausted and asks if I'd mind accompanying her back up and out and to her bedroom. We enter the elevator, because . . . right, there's an elevator I never knew about in my backyard . . . and ride it to the main office, where I glance again at all the instruments and maps there, the colors and sounds. When did she find all these things and drag them here? Everything looks like it weighs two tons. How did she pay for this?

Together we leave the garage, the office, Mother Nature's headquarters pulsing with expectations, and I lock the door behind me with my new key, making sure I can hear the audible *click* of the latch.

Outside, it does look like it rained. Earlier, there wasn't a rain cloud in the sky.

Back in her room, Grandma negotiates her way under the covers, pale and winded after such a long day and night.

"When you have a daughter, you'll pass on this gift as well."

A daughter? I haven't even kissed a guy.

I take Grandma's hand in mine. "I love you," I tell her, even though I don't know what is happening, or why. But no matter what, I do love her, maybe even more now than ever before.

"Happy birthday, my darling," Grandma says. "This is one birthday you'll never forget."

I gently close her door and run upstairs, skipping every other step. I tap on Mom's door, but she doesn't answer. I pound harder with my fist.

"What?" she says angrily. "Resting!"

"Mom, we have to talk about Grandma," I say, waiting for her response.

But there's nothing, just the muffled sound of sheets rustling.

Chapter Three

"Chloe!" Shannon yells from across the quad at school the next day. She's wearing a yellow hoodie. She races over to where I'm standing. I'm a numb and confused zombie operating on zero sleep. I'm worried about Grandma, and I don't want to be here at school. "So? What'd you get?" she asks.

But before I can think of how to answer, I touch the key to the office, which I attached to a chain last night, which I'm now wearing as a necklace.

"Fire!" Shannon says. "Felix guessed it would be jewelry."

"It's not *just* jewelry," I say. "This key belonged to my grandmother."

"What was it a key to? Her house?"

"Yeah," I lie. "The house she grew up in."

"Oh, wow. Like, in the 1800s?"

The thing about Shannon is . . . she's not kidding.

"No," I say, correcting her. "My grandmother was born in the twentieth century."

Shannon looks confused, so I clarify.

"That's the 1900s."

"I know," she says defensively.

"I turned it into a charm."

"It's supercool. It looks like it could unlock a box of secrets."

"Shan?" I start. I want to ask her about dementia. "How's your grandmother doing?"

"Aw, thanks for asking. She thinks she's a pilot and that I'm my mom, but otherwise fine."

I wince. If this is Grandma's future . . .

"Why?" she asks.

"I don't know. I'm a little worried about my grandmother. She was acting super . . . super not like herself yesterday. I don't even know how to explain."

Shannon tilts her head.

"She did this whole dramatic thing at the beach. It doesn't even make sense to describe it."

"Well, maybe your mom should start by taking her to the doctor," Shannon says. "If she hasn't already. It took three doctors before we got a diagnosis."

"Yeah," I say. "I think so, too."

"Felix is getting counseled in Mrs. Boyle's office," Shannon says. "Meet for lunch later?"

I nod.

Was it only twenty-four hours ago that I was sitting in Mrs. Boyle's office myself, strategizing ways to get into a semidecent college?

In English, I sit toward the back of the class and stare out the window. Mr. Rosenberg reads from *As You Like It*, because we're studying Shakespeare's comedies. I don't find them funny, and I'm having a hard time following the plot: Rosalind is Ganymede, Celia is Orlando. Or is Orlando Oliver? Whoever they are, they're giving me a headache.

I fiddle with the key around my neck. I keep picturing the scene at the beach yesterday, Grandma's gentle voice trying to coax me into this unbelievable story about being Mother Nature, and then all the props in the office. I stare past the parking lot, fixing my gaze on the tree-lined streets. The trees. Mother Nature made those trees. Wait, does my grandmother think *she* made those trees? I shake away the thought.

"How is identity a theme of this play?" Mr. Rosenberg asks.

I look behind him, at the board, but he catches my eye.

"Chloe?"

"Oh . . ."

"You're about to say something?"

"No, no," I clarify. "I'm not."

"Yes, yes," he mocks. "I'm asking you to respond. Identity?"

"Identity?" I repeat.

Some classmates giggle.

"That's right," he says, crossing his arms. "What do we know about identity in this play?"

But before I can articulate anything, he's impatiently moving on to someone else.

At lunch, Shannon spreads out on the grass in the middle of the quad, and I think about Grandma's monologue to me about people getting in the way of nature, and how the quad grass requires so much water, since it barely rains here.

"So, who's going to the dance with me next month?" Felix asks. He means the Harvest Dance, the one where they pretend it's East Coast fall in Central California.

"No way," Shannon says.

"I don't do dances," I say.

"Thank you both so much," Felix says. "It's great having friends."

"How was your meeting with Mrs.—" I start. But I feel a hand on my shoulder, and when I turn around, I see Curtis Reed hovering above me, backlit by the sun.

"Hey, happy belated birthday," he says. The sun is blocking his face but not his curly hair.

Surprise, surprise! I'm struck speechless. Again.

"Thanks," I finally stammer. "Thanks so much."

Felix and Shannon are staring into their food. I can see them out of the corner of my eye.

"Lemme move over here," he says. "You're all . . ." And he squints his eyes, imitating me. He steps away from the sun, and I can now see all of him. "So, you're a Libra?" Curtis says, squatting down to join me on the grass.

"Virgo," I say.

"Oh, that's right—September. What's the symbol for Virgo?"

"The virgin," Shannon says, louder than necessary.

"I'm Aries," he says. "April."

"The bull," I say.

"Actually, it's a ram," he says.

It was in Chorus two years ago where Curtis and I met, when I was a freshman and he was a sophomore. Well, it's where I met the back of his head—his thick, wavy black hair. His head bobbed to the music. *Gloria in excelsis Deo, gloria alleluia!* It was the kind of hair that invited you in to touch it, smell it, run your hands through it, but I was too scared to even open the invitation.

It wasn't until I was a sophomore that he acknowledged me, picking up my sheet music when it dropped at his feet. "Here you go, Chloe," he'd said, and I was shocked that he knew my name. I'd written *Curtis and Chloe,* surrounded by hearts, plenty of times—in my notebook, in my journal, on my palm—but when it came time to actual connection, I couldn't muster the courage. I just couldn't believe a cute guy with an easy smile and a great tenor voice could have anything to do with someone like me.

"My birthday's April nineteenth," Curtis says.

Felix taps my foot with his. I think his foot is trying to nudge me to reply. But my mind has gone blankety-blank.

"'April is the cruelest month,'" I say. I know it's from a poem, but I can't remember which one.

"Thanks a lot!" Curtis says.

Under his breath Felix says, "College."

"Oh," I say. "And where are you applying to college?" Maybe a subject change will save this whole conversation.

Shannon stands up and quickly walks away. I think she's laughing, but I can't bring myself to look.

"It's so stressful," Curtis says, rolling his eyes. "You're only a junior, right? So at least you have one more year before it all goes down."

There is a silence between us. I want to fill it, but yet again I have no idea what to say. Who was the poet who said April is the cruelest month?

"Can you believe this weather?" Curtis says, standing up and looking skyward. "It's, like, pouring rain one minute and sunny the next. Global warming, I guess."

"Yeah," I say, picturing my grandmother's finger on mine yesterday, sliding that lever down, down, down. Was it just a coincidence that the rain stopped when she did that?

"*The Waste Land*," Curtis says, smiling. "T. S. Eliot."

That's it! That's the poem and the poet!

When he's gone, I touch my shoulder where his hand rested earlier.

"Oh my lanta," Felix says. "Already talking poetry. So romantic."

"I screwed up," I say. "How did he even know about my birthday? It shocked me so much I didn't know what to say."

"I told him," Shannon confesses as she approaches us again. "Don't kill me. Our moms are in the same book club, remember? He's picked her up at my house a few times."

"I always forget," I say. "I won't kill you, but I just killed an opportunity to have some sort of meaningful conversation with him."

"You were fine," Felix lies. "But maybe next time, don't blink so much."

"Was I blinking?"

"Little bit," Felix says, fluttering his eyelashes.

"Leave her alone," Shannon says, swatting him. "You were fine. The conversation was fine. He's adorable, and so are you. And I think you should finally go for it."

Maybe. I have bigger things to worry about now, though.

Suddenly, a torrent of water soaks us. It's the sprinklers in the quad, going off in the middle of the day, hissing as they spray the grass. A total waste of water. We stand up and run off, along with everyone else who was just trying to enjoy their lunch.

As I enter Chemistry, Mr. Kortege hands each student an envelope and asks us not to open it until he's done taking roll. Then he announces with a sly smile that he's assigned each of us an element from the periodic table, and that once we open our envelope, we have to act out the "personality" of the revealed element for the rest of class—and, preferably, for the rest of the day. "That way, I'll know that you'll at least get one answer right on the midterm."

Not to be paranoid, but I'm positive that he looks right at me when he says it.

"I'm barium!" Tim, the guy next to me, says when he opens his. "I'm a heavy metal!" He sticks his tongue out and shoots two fingers up into the air.

"Arsenic, number thirty-three," Peter calls out. He silently reads from his card and then turns to me and says in a creepy voice, "I kill you!"

I open my envelope to find that I am argon, a noble gas, bone-idle and basically lazy. The card reads: "Totally lackluster."

"Argon," I say weakly to no one in particular. "Number eighteen."

I read on about argon's inert atmosphere. What does Mr. Kortege really know about me anyway? He sees me for one hour a day. I certainly am not going to act out argon—*totally lackluster*—for the rest of the afternoon. I've enrolled in Chemistry, not Drama. Plus, I have better things to do with my time than listen to Magnesium, 12, brag about how easy it is for her to make friends and get reactions.

In the middle of class, I steal away to the bathroom without even asking for permission. I don't understand why I'm on the verge of tears.

I quickly step inside a stall, close the door, and find myself weeping silently into a crumpled wad of toilet paper. I have no idea why I'm crying so hard. It can't just be that I'm lackluster. It's got to be about Grandma, too.

And then—I can tell by the sound of her shoes, the *clickity-clack* of her too-high heels, I know it's Brooklyn Weber before she even opens her mouth.

"OMG, I have food in my teeth!"

"I didn't notice," says the other voice, probably her stupid friend Hailey.

"Oh, it's lipstick," Brooklyn says, relieved. "Next time, please tell me if I have lippy on my teeth."

"I will," Hailey says. "I mean, if I notice."

"What are you even wearing to the dance?" Brooklyn asks. But before Hailey can answer, Brooklyn says, "I bought a vintage dress, and I'm getting my hair done in an updo by Christophe."

"Gonna get your hair done did?" Hailey mocks.

"Um, yeah. I hope you are, too."

"I wasn't planning on it."

"Sweetie, one night. Do yourself a favor."

"Do you guys wanna come over before," Hailey asks, "and we can go together?"

"Well, not really. Curtis is coming to my place and, you know, we'll probably need some private time before making our grand entrance. Plus, my parents won't be home, so I want to maximize make-out time."

Curtis? Make-out time? Make-out time with Curtis? *My* Curtis? Not *my* Curtis! How can it be *my* Curtis? But who else has that name? Now, on top of crying, I want to puke.

Between breaths, I inadvertently let out a sigh, a desperate howl, and then, worse, a loud snort on the inhale. I don't know what's taken over my body.

I hear giggles from outside the stall, and then the sound of those pointy heels trotting away.

"What the hell?" I hear Brooklyn's voice say on her way out. "Was there some sort of animal in there?"

Her stupid friend cackles and then exaggeratedly imitates my snort.

No matter how much water I splash on my face, the puff around my eyes is still visible. The face staring back at me is not mine—how can it be? Or maybe this is what I've always looked like and this is the first time I'm really *seeing*. This matted brown hair, all asymmetrical and chunky, is not hair that Christophe would put in an *updo*—whoever he is and whatever that is. This is not a face that Curtis Reed could fall in love with. I stare at myself in disbelief—maybe I really am argon, an inert element.

I'm so lost in thought that I don't even notice the *clickity-clack* returning, but suddenly I see Brooklyn in the mirror, behind me. There is a solitary tube of lipstick in front of me.

"Excuse me," she says, reaching over for it.

I'm shocked she's managed to utter that pleasantry.

She picks up her lipstick and then looks at me. "Wait. You didn't touch this, did you?"

For some reason, I say, "Touch or use?" though, of course, I'd done neither.

"Touch," she clarifies.

"No," I say pointedly.

She grabs the lipstick and, on the way out of the bathroom, tosses it into the trash can. I can hear the solitary *plink* it makes, landing at the bottom.

No, I think. *No, you're not getting away with another insult. You're not allowed to suggest that my even looking at your ugly lipstick is enough to warrant throwing it away.* There is no way I'm allowing that wretched girl to have make-out time with my curly-haired crush.

"I'm going to the dance with you," I shout as I run past Felix on my way back to Chemistry to get my backpack.

"You hate dances," he reminds me.

"Not anymore."

Chapter Four

At home after school, I slip in through the front door and run upstairs to my room, where I'm determined to research some doctors for Grandma. My purple journal catches my eye. I pull it from the shelf and thumb through the pages, stopping on my last entry, from early August, when I was complaining about going bathing-suit shopping. At the top of the page, I'd graded the day a D. I grab a blue pen from my desk and flip to the next empty page:

I know it's been a month, and I really have no excuse, but now I need to write. I don't even know where to start, or how to explain what has transpired over the last 24 hours. I guess I'll just get it down the easiest way possible:

- *Curtis wished me a happy birthday in person. IN PERSON. I fumbled through some sort of conversation with him, trying hard to keep eye contact, and it wasn't perfect, but I think we lasted about 5 minutes—a record for us. Well, for me.*
- *(I turned 16 since the last time I wrote in here, which is why he wished me a happy birthday in the first place.)*
- *Grandma's having some sort of delusional ~~halluca- halucinn-~~ hallucinations, or however you spell it. She thinks she's Mother Nature. She's done a whole thing in the garage, pretending it's headquarters or something. Confused? Well, imagine how I feel. Looking up specialists now because she needs her head checked ASAP.*
- *Mom's a bitch.*

Love, Chloe

Grandma knows I'm home, because I hear her call up, "Are you ready for your first official tutorial, honey?"

"Maybe later," I yell back. "I have to study for my English quiz." But really, I'm about to Google "What to do if you think a loved one has dementia."

I hear footsteps climbing the stairs, and then Grandma appears and takes my hand. "Nothing in your English class is as important as this," she insists, leading me out of my room before I even have a chance to type anything into the search bar.

I reluctantly follow her back down the stairs, and together we head outside. She walks with me, arm in arm. "Come," she says, guiding me to the lemon tree behind the office.

Oh gosh, I think. *Now what?*

"This is premature for you, but I want you to see something dazzling," she says.

She positions herself in front of the tree and calls out, "Crescere arbor," and she lifts her hands like she's about to conduct an orchestra. "Crescere arbor!" she says again—in a booming voice, so loud I'm sure the neighbors can hear.

Suddenly, little yellow buds start blooming on the branches. Then, all over the tree, like popcorn popping, the buds burst into bright-yellow lemons.

Right in front of me.

"Oh my God!" I shriek. "How is this—? What are you—?"

Grandma lets out a hearty laugh.

"Remember when you were a little girl? And—"

"And I sold lemonade in the driveway because there were so many lemons?" One summer, I made fifty dollars in a day, because it was so hot outside and everybody was stopping to buy something to drink.

I stare at the tree, the thorny branches now weighed down by clusters of golden-yellow fruits, some the size of tennis balls, others the size of baseballs. Then I stare at my grandmother.

"You're going to catch flies, dear," she says about my hanging jaw.

But I don't close it. Instead, I take a step closer to the tree, inspecting it. What am I looking for, exactly? Some elaborate contraption? I tug a lemon off, and the whole tree shakes. I inhale deeply. Yup, it smells like citrus. "Grandma," I say, "what big lemons you have."

"Pretty nifty, huh?" she says, taking it from me. "The better to make lemonade with. Anyway, growing lemons is far down the line for you, but I thought it would put a smile on your face to see what your future holds."

She takes me into her arms, her smell so familiar, like grass and snow and vanilla, and now lemon. She whispers into my ear, "Let's step inside."

Okay, not only does she *think* she's Mother Nature . . . Now *I* think she's Mother Nature! Or at least that she *might* be. I'm trying to understand. I'm trying to make this make sense.

She has me unlock the door, and we take the elevator down. She leads me over to the hologram of Earth spinning in the center of the space. Or is it me who's spinning?

"Look carefully," she says. "What do you see?"

I see that the giant globe is suspended, and I don't get what technology would allow for this, but it's beautiful, with the neon-blue oceans and vast green lands.

"Look closer," Grandma instructs, and I step forward. I see little red markers pulsating at various frequencies throughout the globe.

"Can you see what's happening over Switzerland?" she asks, and I gaze in the general direction of Europe, afraid to tell her I don't know exactly where Switzerland is. Grandma steps in closer and follows my gaze. "That's Argentina, dear," she says. "Switzerland." She points to the actual spot, way up and to the right. I identify the red marker, quivering in a way the others aren't.

"I see," I say.

"Now, Zurich?" she says, pointing closer.

"It's shaking." I mimic the movement with my finger.

"It's the earth demanding the release of pressure," she says.

"How do you know?"

"Over sixty-five years on the job, dear."

She writes some notes on a pad of paper and then circles the globe, jotting down data. I follow her to the farthest wall of the office, where maps blink and sparkle for attention. She types something into a computer and then announces that she has just set in motion the beginnings of an earthquake to release the pressure in Zurich.

"What?"

"If I could catch them all at this stage," she says, "we could avoid the catastrophic ones."

Right. Because that's what Mother Nature does.

"When will it happen?" I ask.

"Within twelve hours," she says. "In Zurich. But you saw all the blinking. Those are *all* earthquakes in a fledgling state."

Fledgling: noun, a state of emergence. As in: Apparently, I'm a fledgling Mother Nature.

"But there are hundreds," I say, looking closer.

"Honey, there are *thousands*."

I start thinking about all the recent disasters, or at least the ones in my lifetime. The earthquake in Iran? Oh my God. The tsunami in Indonesia?

"You've got to be so careful," she explains. "Pretend that this is a roomful of the most delicate glassware you can imagine. Pretend, for now, you're in a museum."

We spend the next four hours together, monitoring the boards, reading *The Book of Nature*, my brain trying desperately to process everything.

At first, I was pretending to believe she was Mother Nature, but I don't think I'm pretending anymore.

Later that night, I make myself mac and cheese and watch *Jeopardy!* alone in the den. I want to distract myself from everything, and TV is the best way I know how. The category is "Oceans."

"This is the biggest animal in the ocean," the host says.

I call out, "Shark!"

"What is the blue whale?" a contestant says.

"That's right," the host says.

"'Need For Speed' for two hundred," the same contestant says.

"This animal can run up to seventy miles per hour."

"What is a bobcat!" I call.

"What is a cheetah?" the contestant answers.

"That's correct."

I scoop another spoonful of noodles into my mouth.

At a commercial break, Duncan Sunshine appears on the screen. "Just getting news of a 6.2 earthquake in Zurich, Switzerland," he says to the camera. "So unusual in that part of the world. Lots of rocking and rolling, but no injuries reported at this time. Stay tuned for the news at ten."

I drop my spoon into the bowl. The *clank* echoes in the quiet house.

Earthquake.

Switzerland.

Just as Grandma predicted. No wait—just as Grandma *made happen*.

I swallow hard, digesting my new reality, along with a spoonful of undercooked noodles. I inhale sharply, and forget to exhale. I set my bowl down, and head back to the office to see what else Grandma has in store.

Chapter Five

It's not that I'm ungrateful I'm becoming Mother Nature. It's just that . . . let's be honest . . . I'm the last person in the world who should be bestowed such a gift. (a) I said it before, but it bears repeating—I have this weird thing against sand. And shouldn't Mother Nature naturally embrace all the elements? (b) I care about the environment, really I do, but last year it was Brooklyn Weber who spearheaded this school-wide campaign to save the penguins, and I didn't even contribute. I don't hate penguins or anything; it was solely because I hate Brooklyn. But still (c) I want to go to college. I *have* to go to college. I have to be better than my own two parents and get out of my small town. And (d) wasn't I just assigned argon—one of the most inert elements on the periodic table?

On a Saturday morning in early October, Grandma tells me more about the transition period, which really only happens once every twenty to forty-five years. "If you look back in history, you can see a pattern emerge. 1965. Hurricane Betsy. That was my elbow mistakenly setting off a switch."

What can I say but, "Whoopsie."

"I felt so awful. The technology was new, and I was clumsy. Today, however, we're going to talk about the concept of symmetry."

Symmetry: noun, the quality of being made up of exactly similar parts facing each other or around an axis. Another word on the ACT vocabulary list.

"Now, let's look at this wall," she says, walking me over to the one closest to the elevator. It's glowing amber.

"This is an important screen for you, Chloe. These are the impending natural disasters, and we're going to get to those in the next few days, after you read the chapter on it. This is something you're going to have to check daily. Do you understand?"

"Totally," I say. "Check daily."

She gazes at me.

"You're speaking as though the tutorial will be done in a couple of hours, but Chloe, this will most likely take a few years."

"Years?"

"Of course, darling. Years."

I quietly listen as she walks me through other countries and continents and control panels. We study Bolivia, Argentina, Greenland. After another hour and a half, Grandma says she's tired and needs a nap. She tells me, "Remember this: Nature will always follow its course, just like a teenager. You can intervene, but only when absolutely necessary, like a good mother."

A good mother.

What do I know about that?

"We'll meet again tonight," she tells me. "Seven o'clock."

But tonight's the Harvest Dance.

I explain the situation to Grandma in the hopes she'll understand. She seems frustrated, but I have a fun idea.

"Can we make things windy tonight? Like superblustery but not a tornado?" All I know is I want to blow that Christophe hairdo off Brooklyn's horrible head. I gaze around at all the instruments, trying to intuit which one controls the wind.

"Darling!" Grandma says. "What are you talking about?"

"I don't even know how she knows him," I start. "I've been in Chorus with him for years, and now *she's* suddenly dating him?"

"A boy." Grandma nods.

"Not just a boy," I explain. "*Curtis.*"

"A boy named Curtis," Grandma says.

"Can you please make it windy tonight?" I beg.

"Chloe," Grandma says. "We don't manipulate our powers for self-serving purposes." She walks to the bank of levers and screens by the back wall. I follow quickly behind. "Wind is the result of shifting airstreams. You don't simply 'make' wind."

"Well, then how do I shift airstreams?" I ask.

"You're not going to let up, are you?" She sighs. "Look, these are the atmospheric maps. Do you see the different white wisps across the board?"

"Yeah."

"I want you to touch one of the lower streams with your ring finger. And make sure it's your ring finger, because it exerts the least pressure. Why don't you locate Minnesota and do it there? Now slowly guide it upward."

I do as I'm told—first, searching the map for Minnesota and, once finding it, placing my finger on the screen. The airstream follows my finger as I drag it to the top of the screen. And when I let go, it stays there.

"Okay," Grandma says. "You just caused a windstorm over Minneapolis."

"No way."

"You moved warm air to the top of the atmosphere, and therefore the cold air moved in automatically in its place."

"How cool is that?"

"It's *cool,*" Grandma says. "Now, if you were to quickly reverse that action, that would be a monsoon."

"It's that easy?"

"I want you to study the Beaufort scale in *The Book of Nature*, somewhere around page three hundred and twenty, if I remember correctly," she says. "Also around there, you'll see the different types of winds: Sirocco, Chinook, Santa Ana."

"Oh! I know Santa Ana! The warm winds!"

"That's right," she says.

"I love those."

"So do I. And soon you'll learn how to produce them," she says.

I think back to all of the nights Grandma and I sat out in the backyard talking, me lifting my head like a dog to catch the warm wind against my face.

"Tell me more about the boy named Curtis," Grandma says.

"Well, he's smart, and he's got this great, curly head of hair. And his singing voice! It's like . . . it's like . . . Frank Sinatra."

"Sinatra!" Grandma says. "That's some compliment!"

"He's not a jock. He's not a jerk. He's not a nerd. He's a senior. And, Grandma, I feel like *I* discovered him, and then Brooklyn just swept him right up from under me!"

"Brooklyn's a person?" Grandma asks.

I nod.

"Who's named after a borough?"

"Exactly."

Grandma looks at me—her steel-blue eyes intense. "A little wind tonight, you say?"

I nod, hopeful.

"In the name of love?"

"Well, I don't know if I'd call it—"

"In the name of love," she says, interrupting me. "I suppose it wouldn't hurt anyone. But let's not make this a habit." She winks. "Understand, dear?"

For the past year, I've been counting down the days to when I could get my driver's license. All I've ever wanted is the freedom that a car seems to allow—the chance to get out of my house, away from my neighborhood, past Morro Bay and its giant, looming rock. I watched, biting my nails to the nub, as Brooklyn was publicly gifted her Mercedes in front of the entire school last year. But now that I'm becoming Mother Nature, how can I contribute to all the pollution that Grandma has been raging about—oil and everything else? I simply can't. I know there are electric and hybrid cars, but last night, in the middle of the night when I couldn't sleep, I did some research and found out they can be bad for the environment, too.

Felix drives a Prius, and Shannon drives a Jeep. I always sat in their back seats, fantasizing about the car I would eventually drive. But it's clear that I can't contribute to the nitrogen oxides and the reactive hydrocarbons destroying the planet. And how could I ever afford a car, let alone an electric one?

So I go on Craigslist to look for bikes.

I bookmark a few options, and when Grandma takes a nap, I text the owner of a "good as new" bicycle. Not only is it affordable; it's available. And the house is only a fifteen-minute walk away from mine. We decide to meet at three o'clock.

At two thirty, I walk over to check out the bike. As I amble down the block, I think I see flowers shooting out of the ground as I pass—yellow, lavender, and cream poppies in one yard, soft pink roses in another. It must be my imagination, or some sort of optical illusion.

But as I walk farther, I realize it's truly happening. Yellow-and-white daisies spring from someone's front garden, just like in a pop-up children's book. I approach the flowers and smile. Perhaps this is some sort of reward for becoming Mother Nature? As pretty as it is, I walk faster, because it's also kind of freaking me out.

Soon, I'm surrounded by houses with circular driveways and sprawling front yards. I've always wondered who lived in this neighborhood. I ring the bell at the address from the text, and a ten-year-old opens the door.

"Hi," I say to her. "Is your mom or dad home? I'm here to look at the bike."

"It's *my* bike," she snaps. "You don't need my parents."

"Oh, I'm sorry," I say, about to walk away. "I'm actually looking for a grown-up bike."

"Chill," the kid says. "Let me show it to you before you bail." And she closes the door.

A minute later, she emerges from the side of her house with the cutest bicycle I've ever seen—pale yellow with red painted flowers, and a little basket between the handlebars.

"Oh my God," I say. "It's adorable!"

"I know," she says. "It's, like, too cutesy for me."

"Can I give it a spin?"

"Sure. Do you need me to raise the seat?"

How embarrassing that I don't, that I'm actually the same size as this kid. "I think I'm good," I say, hopping on and biking around in her circular driveway.

I try the bell on the handlebar. *Ring, ring!* The sound soothes and delights me. "I think I'll take it," I say.

"You think? Or you will?"

"Will," I say. "I'll take it."

"I accept crypto," the kid says.

"I actually have cash," I respond, and she looks crestfallen.

I hand over the crisp hundred-dollar bill that Grandma gave me earlier when she heard about my decision not to drive. I press the bill into her hand.

"Did you have fish for breakfast or something?" she asks me, closing her fist around the cash.

"No! Why? Does my breath stink?" It's possible that with everything going on, I'd forgotten to brush my teeth. I cover my mouth with my palm and try to smell my own breath.

"No, but . . ." She points behind me, and when I turn, I see about a dozen cats approaching and meowing.

"What the—?" I say. They're slinking toward me, staring intently with their green eyes. Is this another gift from the natural world for becoming Mother Nature, a welcome-to-the-job party attended only by . . . cats?

"This is too weird, Cat Girl," the kid says, backing into her house.

Before she slams her front door, I say a quick goodbye. Then I hop on the bike and start pedaling, sounding the bell so all those cats will quit following me. I pedal home as fast as the wind.

Chapter Six

"I'm going with you because Brooklyn's dating Curtis," I confess to Felix as I climb into his Prius while trying not to expose my undies in my short black knit skirt.

"Liar!" Felix says. "In what universe would those two connect?"

"Swear to God," I say, buckling up. "I know for a fact."

"What are you, some sort of sadist? You actually *want* to see your frenemy—"

"No 'f-r,'" I say. "Flat-out *enemy*."

"You want to see your *flat-out enemy* with the love of your life, that you can barely form words in front of? We're going tonight so you can . . . what . . . pour punch down her dress? Trip her? Beat her in a dance-off?"

"How is it possible that out of all the guys in our school, she picked him?"

"Maybe he picked her."

"No way," I say. Because even though I don't really know him, I know him well enough to know he didn't pick her. He couldn't have. But I don't say this out loud, because I realize how it would make me sound.

"You know what I think?" he says. "I think you need to focus all your energy on learning how to actually *talk* to Curtis. I think the only thing Brooklyn has over you is that *she* talks to him and *you* don't."

"I try!" I say. "I just always flub it."

We ride the rest of the way to school in silence—not because I am mad, but because I think he has a point.

Felix looks disappointed as we approach the parking lot. "So, that's the *only* reason you're coming with me tonight?"

"No, no!" I say. "I'm coming because we always have a good time together."

At least that part is true.

Shannon and I met Felix in the cafeteria in seventh grade. He'd just transferred to our school and was using mashed potatoes to describe what his new house looked like, carving the front door and windows with a knife, and even smoothing out the potatoes to show the attic. And if that wasn't good enough, he poured gravy through the potato chimney and ate the whole thing up. I loved him from the get-go.

The gym has a few haystacks thrown in the corner, some

hanging pumpkin lights, and stalks of dried corn scattered about, in a meager but earnest attempt at a harvest theme. I am immediately uncomfortable when we walk in; this is so not my scene. My classmates are mostly milling around outside because it's a warm night, but the diehards are already inside and on the dance floor.

"I see them," Felix says in a resigned tone, and when I look in his direction, I see them, too. Brooklyn is laughing in her black strapless dress, and then suddenly she's tucked into Curtis like a little bird, then laughing again. I watch her hand as she raises it to his hair and runs her fingers through his curls. She then takes his hand and leads him outside.

I know it is time for me to strike. I send a text to Grandma: Ready, set, wind!

In five minutes the first gust kicks up and I run outside. Brooklyn's dress billows up and out, exposing her purple panties. Leaves flutter off trees, and then trees start bending. Someone's drink cup flies out of their hand and bounces its way across the cement. I picture Grandma in the office orchestrating it all.

I watch in delight as Brooklyn's hair starts blowing out of its tightly fastened bobby pins. "Aaah!" she screams, trying to manage it all, her drink cup, her flapping dress, her loose strands of hair wild in the wind. She laughs amidst the chaos, and with her tousled hair and beaming smile she looks like she's some sort of supermodel heading down the runway.

Then before I know it, an umbrella topples out of its stand, nearly gouging Curtis in the abdomen as it flies past.

Oops.

I hear a chorus of "Ohhhs" from everyone nearby.

"That was so scary!" Brooklyn says, running toward Curtis. "Are you okay?"

He nods as she rubs his stomach.

Trees are blowing around violently when a branch falls off and lands beside my feet.

Mr. Kortege, my Chem teacher, appears in the doorway of the gym. "Everybody inside now," he commands. Grandma's really laying it on thick!

I stand watching as students file inside. "Chloe Lovejoy!" he yells. "Do you want to get killed?"

"Let's go," Brooklyn says urgently, taking Curtis's hand.

"Where?" Hailey asks, trying to steady her balance.

"My house. The parentals won't be home for at least another two hours." Then she calls to her other friends, "After-party, my house!"

"But we just got here," Curtis says.

Brooklyn doesn't answer him. She keeps a firm grip on his hand and drags him to the parking lot.

I watch, deflated, as they disappear into the blustery night.

Then, seemingly out of the blue, it's not only blustery; it's raining. A little at first, and then harder and harder still. And . . . what the . . . Hail? Frozen rain is pelting my skin. I see lightning in the distance, but I don't hear thunder.

I race to the doorway as the storm rages. The hail sounds like the thunderous applause of a packed audience. And then . . . Snow? In Morro Bay?

I reach for my phone to text Grandma that she can stop now, she can lay off, but when I pull my phone out of my pocket, I see that I have a text: EMERGENCY. COME HOME IMMEDIATELY.

From . . . my dad? I think this is only the second text I've ever received from him, the other being Does this thing work? when he first got his phone.

I respond: Okay?!?

The howling wind doesn't stop; in fact, it's gaining speed. Snowflakes are blowing everywhere. It looks like a blizzard.

I run inside and make my way across the gym, my heart hammering as I search desperately for Felix. I find him on the dance floor, entertaining the crowd with the Electric Slide.

"I need to get home," I say breathlessly when I reach him.

Felix dismisses me by waving his hands in the air to the beat of the music, but when I burst into uncontrollable tears, he finally takes notice.

Please, I mouth, and he moves away from the crowd to join me.

"Was it that bad seeing them together?" he says, putting an arm around me.

"It's windy and hailing and snowing!"

"Snowing?" Felix says.

"Also, there's some sort of emergency at home," I say, holding up my phone so he can see my dad's text, but the screen has already defaulted to my screen saver. "Just trust me. Please?"

He grabs my hand, and together we dash out to his car, but now the weather is even more powerful than I expected it to be.

"I don't know if I can drive in this," Felix says.

"You have to," I beg, so he starts the engine and we head out into the elements.

There's an ambulance parked in my driveway when we arrive, its red lights spinning in the black night.

God, is it my mother? Did she trip and hit her head on the stove like she did once before?

"Oh, Chloe," Felix says, putting the car in park. "Do you want me to come in with you?"

"It's okay," I say, hopping out. I don't even say goodbye or thank you; I just run to the front door.

My dad is standing there, with a frantic expression.

"What the— Where's Mom?" I ask.

"With her," Dad says.

"With who?" I ask, and Dad shakes his head.

I run back to Grandma's room. "What is going o—?" I start. But there are two medics in there, and suddenly I know what's going on. "She can't die!" I insist. "She's not dying! Is she? She can't!"

"She did," my mom says as the medics cover Grandma's body with a single white sheet.

"No!" I say.

"She collapsed in the office. I knew something was wrong when I heard hail pelting my window," Mom says in a low whisper, acknowledging our shared secret.

"Heart attack or stroke," a paramedic tells me, seemingly unfazed by what my mom just said. Both medics look at me sadly and sweetly, expressing their condolences.

"No," I repeat. "No, no, no, no."

"Chloe, get ahold of yourself," Mom says as she follows the paramedics down the hallway with Grandma's lifeless body on the gurney.

I hear muted, concerned talk between my mom and dad, but I can't make out the specifics, and I can't seem to move. I fall into Grandma's bed—her grassy, citrus scent still alive on the pillows.

How on earth is this happening? Is it my fault? In asking for wind, did I inadvertently set off some awful process that resulted in her death?

Grandma had made it clear she shouldn't use her powers for personal gain, but she did it anyway—her final living gesture—for me. And now . . . and now . . .

My tears are as steady as the rain outside, and I have no idea how to stop either.

Chapter Seven

"C'mon," Mom says, motioning for me to stand up. "We need to get going in the office."

I look up at her and instinctively touch the key, which is resting against my collarbone. I'm still in Grandma's room. I don't know what time it is, but it's the middle of the night. I must have fallen asleep. "We?" I say.

"Up," she says, trying to peel me off Grandma's bed. But I'm not ready to move. I feel like deadweight.

"Mom," I say groggily. "I'll go later."

"But the storm," she says. "It can't go on like this all night."

"I'll figure it out," I tell her, annoyed that for once she's acting like a responsible adult.

"Oh, okay, you know everything," she says, walking out. She mumbles something about Grandma passing her over and how it was the worst decision in the world.

Later, much later, in the early hours of dawn, I use my key to unlatch the lock to the office and enter the room tentatively. I close the door behind me.

The maps twinkle and blip, and when I take the elevator down, the hologram of Earth spins in the middle of the room. Even though Grandma's been training me for weeks, suddenly everything seems foreign and overwhelming again, like the first time I stepped in here on the evening of my birthday, when I thought she was losing her mind. My breathing is loud and heavy. Everything is pulsing for Grandma's attention.

No, *my* attention.

I'm Mother Nature, I tell myself. *I'm Mother Nature now.*

But I don't believe it. How can I? A few hours ago, I was at the Harvest Dance, and I couldn't even manage a simple hello to the guy I like.

I approach the rain panels, the ones Grandma showed me just the other day, the ones she must have collapsed in front of, and I'm able to move the lever down, down, down, stopping the dramatic rain outside. Then I locate Central California on the wind screen. If triggering the wind in the first place was a finger swipe upward, does that mean swiping the opposite way will end this blustery mess? What did Grandma say about a monsoon? I don't know the answer, or at least I don't remember, so

I consult *The Book of Nature*, which is behind the glass on the shelf below the intercom.

As I open the delicate pages, I feel panic set in. I thumb through the browning paper until I find the specific chapter, halfway through the book, on wind, along with illustrations and graphs and a handwritten addition from Grandma in the margins. There is a technique to stopping wind, and it's not just a finger swipe down. Instead, I have to make a gentle circular motion in the air, before swiping down on the wind screen and then ceasing the force of the gusts.

I look from the book to the panel and back again, reading and rereading the information until I'm 100 percent clear that this is what I must do.

Then, I do it.

I ride the elevator back up.

The windows aren't rattling anymore. Nothing is dropping onto the roof.

There is so much to read, so much to learn. The thought is so overwhelming that I want to crawl under my covers, like I usually do on the heaviest of homework days. But I can't. This is a new reality, and in it, I am Mother Nature.

I emerge from the Maparium two hours later. My eyes feel raw from crying and lack of sleep. Mom's sitting in the dark in the living room, with a gin and something in hand, her drink of choice. "I have a headache," she says. "In case you're wondering why the lights are out."

"Then why are you drinking, Mom?"

"To take the edge off," she says. "I just lost my mother, remember?"

I roll my eyes, but I doubt she can see, since it's so dark.

She tells me Grandma's being cremated and there will be a funeral next Sunday, when we'll scatter her ashes up on Mount Kismo.

"What?" I say, surprised. "Already?"

"Whatever you do, make sure the weather's decent over the weekend."

Grandma always said she wanted to be laid to rest on Mount Kismo, about forty-five miles from our house. She used to ski and hike there when she was younger—neither of which I can picture her doing, but I love the idea.

"What time do you—?" I start.

"Headache," my mom reminds me, holding up her hand.

I take the seat next to her. "How'd this happen?" I ask. "I mean, without warning. Nothing. Just . . . she's . . . here one minute, gone the next?"

"She hadn't been feeling well for a few months."

"*Months?*" I think about all the naps she'd been taking recently. How she'd tired easily and retreated to her room more than I ever remembered.

"She refused to see a doctor. Said she didn't have time. She thought she was above doctors."

"But didn't you try—"

"Don't," she says, raising her voice. "Please. I don't want to hear it. She was a force, and I couldn't reckon with her."

"Sorry for caring," I say, standing up. And before she can retort, I walk out of the living room.

I squint when the light in the hallway hits me. Mom might want to sit there drinking in the dark, but I'm starving, so I head into the kitchen to make myself some sort of breakfast.

I take my food upstairs, grab my purple journal, and mark the top of the page with a giant black F–.

Grandma died.

I can't believe I just wrote those two words, but it's true. Nothing seems real. I don't understand how I kissed her goodbye when I left for the dance one minute and the next she was gone. How am I expected to continue doing anything without her? And I don't just mean the Mother Nature stuff. I mean the life stuff. I just want to give her one last hug. I just want to erase this day. I'm too tired to keep writing. I think I'm even too tired to cry.

More later, I promise.

Love, Chloe

After I brush my teeth, I walk into Mom's room and find her changing into pj's.

"Can I invite Felix to Grandma's funeral next week?" I ask.

"I don't think it's appropriate to bring a date to my mother's funeral."

"A date?" I say in disbelief. "Felix is one of my best friends."

"Uch," Mom says quickly. "Fine."

"And what about Shannon?" I ask.

"Enough," she says, motioning me out of her room.

I'm assuming that's a no. And for what reason? I'm too tired to even ask.

Walking back to my room, the house already feels so lonely.

Chapter Eight

"Chloe!" Shannon yells from across the quad. She races over to where I'm standing, fiddling with my locker. She throws her arms around me and rocks me back and forth. "Felix told me. How are you doing?"

"Not good."

"How'd she die? Was it dementia?"

I shake my head no. "She didn't have that after all. It was totally out of the blue. A stroke or something."

"It sucks to be old," Shannon says. "Actually, it kind of sucks to be young, too."

"It sucks even more to be dead," I say, and she agrees.

I slouch into Life Skills, not in the mood to talk to anyone or see anyone, let alone hear anyone else's problems. Life Skills is our school's version of group therapy, though no one ever calls it that.

This isn't the kind of class where I can hide in the back row and mope, because here we're required to sit on the floor in a circle. Sometimes we talk freely about anything that's on our minds, and sometimes we engage in team-building exercises in an earnest attempt to get us to bond. I watch from the corner of my eye as Brooklyn dramatically steps through the circle and squeezes in between two classmates.

When we are all settled, Ms. Hampton, the facilitator, announces that today we're going to write down anonymous questions, which she will pick from a hat and read, and then discuss them as a group. There are three guidelines we must always abide by, as she reminds us each week: (1) Speak from the heart. (2) Listen from the heart. (3) Don't judge.

"Anything goes," she says as she passes around scraps of paper. "So don't hold back."

I uncap my pen, surprised at how quickly a question comes to mind. I don't even really think about it; I just write. I watch my classmates scribbling down their questions. *How many people have just lost their grandmother?* I wonder.

When everyone has turned in a question, Ms. Hampton digs into the hat, extracts the first folded paper, and reads: "My Mercedes G500 says premium gas only, but what happens if I use regular?"

Tim Thompson immediately raises his hand and begins to mansplain the difference between the two types of gas, something about the blend of hydrocarbons. I'd rather be sleeping than listening to him drone on, but I try hard to withhold my judgment, as required by guideline number three.

"So ultimately, it's in your best interest to use premium," he says. He looks at Brooklyn, whose question it obviously is, and then quickly looks at his lap. "Whoever you are."

Leave it to her to drive a gas guzzler when she pretends to be such an environmental activist. I hate everything about her, but especially this. And especially today.

The next question is about college. "My parents are pressuring me about going to college, but I'm pretty sure I want to take a gap year. How do I talk to them about this? I know they're going to freak."

"A year off?" Brooklyn says. "Why would anyone want to do that?"

Ms. Hampton jumps in. "Right, Brooklyn. That's probably what this person's parents are going to say upon hearing that news."

I raise my hand.

"Chloe?" Ms. Hampton says.

"Maybe they can write a letter to their parents—"

"I don't think that's a good idea," Brooklyn says. "That's avoiding a confrontation. It's passive-aggressive. Words are better spoken in person."

"If you'd let me finish," I say tightly. "Maybe a letter can help clarify the points that this student needs to make in person."

I notice Brooklyn shaking her head no.

I look at the clock, eager to get home and study the weather boards and *The Book of Nature*. I have to practice balancing the world, but I'm stuck in here arguing with Brooklyn Weber.

Suddenly, Ms. Hampton pulls out the next paper and reads my question: "How long does grief last?" She purses her lips, looking around the room. "I'll start by saying that grief takes many forms," she says gently. "Would anybody else like to speak on this?"

I'm shocked by how many hands are raised.

"I slept a lot when my aunt died last year," someone says.

"I ate a lot when my dad died."

"I'm still sad about my cat, who died six years ago."

There are so many losses in this room alone, from pets to parents, and everyone with a slightly different experience. I am grateful for their answers, taking in all their memories and suggestions. I never realized Life Skills could be so comforting.

After school, I arrive to a quiet house. Who knows where Mom is. Today, alone in the house, Grandma's room feels so empty. Those moments with her seem so far away. I open her closet door and reach in for her blue uniform. It still smells so distinctly like her. I take it off the hanger and step into it, fitting it over my clothes. It's too big for me, but I want to wear it.

I leave her room and make my way to the office, trying to remember what she said about all the things I need to know. I should have taken notes. I should have at least recorded her on my iPhone. I should have listened more carefully. Instead, I'd pretended to hear. I'd pretended to understand. It was the best acting I've ever done in my life.

In the Maparium, I take the elevator down and wheel myself over to *The Book of Nature*, carefully taking it from the shelf and gently turning its pages. But I can't even get through a Shakespeare play. How am I going to get through this, alone and without my mentor?

I roll to the bank of levers that controls the rain. It's like I'm in a recording studio or something. There are the levers, but there are also illuminated buttons—some blinking red, some static. I identify Canada and slide the levers up in Vancouver, Banff, Winnipeg, and Hamilton—because why not? Because I can. In Costa Rica, I slide down the levers, so it is no longer raining in San José or over Arenal.

Okay, I'm getting this rain stuff. In fact, it feels so easy that deep down I know I must be doing it wrong somehow. I have to be doing something wrong. I always am.

When I glance at the clock, I see it's a little past four, and I'm in the mood to watch something mindless on TV. I hop off the chair, but my foot gets caught on a wheel, and I slide backward, slamming into the bank of levers and ricocheting toward a map on the opposite wall. I clutch the chair to steady my balance and gaze around helplessly.

Nothing seems out of place; nothing seems destroyed.

I'll get back to *The Book of Nature* eventually, but for now I slink out of the office and back to Grandma's room, where I can pretend things are still normal. I crawl onto her bed and turn on the TV. I try to keep my eyes open as I search for something to watch. But then . . . But then . . .

I wake with a start. I've been sleeping, and I have no idea how much time has passed, but Duncan Sunshine is on TV, next to a weather map that's zooming in on Washington state. "Mother Nature's sure got one on us," he says excitedly. "Aside from wild weather here in Morro Bay, there's unusual seismic activity at Mount Adams." He points to the location of the volcano. "Experts are weighing in on evacuations. Stay tuned for the news at six."

Unusual activity at Mount Adams? I tear off the covers and race back outside, and into the office. Once I identify Washington on the giant map, I see a cluster of blinking orange lights over what seems to be a mountain range. I didn't notice them before. Did I do that?

The blinking intensifies, and I run to *The Book of Nature*, quickly looking up the table of contents: "Making the Transition," "Floods," "Hurricanes," "Lightning," "Thunder," "Tidal Waves" . . .

By the time I reach "Volcanoes," the noise in the room has intensified, the steady pulse of the *beep beep*s quickening. I need help. *Grandma! What am I supposed to do?*

The chapter is long and dense, and I'm speed-reading to no avail, because soon the frantic beeping gives way to a steady hum, like someone's flatlined in a hospital bed, and then, suddenly, there's a silence that makes everything feel unreal. Well, more unreal than it already feels. The blinking orange lights are now void of any color—they're not green, not blue, just burned-out and blunted.

There are flat-screen TVs all in a row hanging from the ceiling. Some are small while others are extra-large, and I wonder if any of them have cable. I push the power button on what looks like a remote. One of the screens blinks on, and Duncan Sunshine is talking excitedly again.

"This has been probably twenty years in the making," he says. "Let's go to our correspondent in the Pacific Northwest. Jessica Nova, what are you seeing?" I watch the screen as white ash covers the reporter, and even floats over the camera lens. "Duncan," she says, "it's just chaos here outside of Portland, Oregon. With little warning, this dormant volcano came to life in an aggressive and unusual fashion."

I look from side to side, feeling the walls of the office closing in on me. I hear my own breathing, which sounds like I've been running a marathon. I shake my head no. I open my mouth, but nothing comes out.

I walk into the kitchen, where Mom is boiling rice—a glass of wine in one hand, a wooden spoon in the other. "A volcano?" she says. "Really?"

"Mother. Stop. Not now."

"Right. It's your life. You know what you're doing. Blah blah blah." She takes a look at me in Grandma's uniform. "You look ridiculous in that," she tells me. "It's five sizes too big on you."

"I like it," I say.

"By the way, I have news. I took a job," she announces. "In marketing."

She's spent her life hopping from job to job—sales, hostess, assistant, management. They usually end in "It just wasn't the right fit," and then she's home for months on end, staying in bed too long and watching too much TV. When Grandpa died, he left some property to her, his only child. She sold it when she was in her late twenties, allowing her the freedom to start and quit jobs. But even I know the money's gonna run out eventually.

"Did you hear me?" she says. "I said I took a job in marketing."

"Supermarketing?" I ask.

"Marketing a new brand of bottled water," she says. "For a startup company."

"Bottled water is terrible for the environment," I tell her. "You know that."

"A 'Congratulations' would have been nice."

"Congratulations."

"It'll be long hours," she says. "But don't worry. There will always be enough food in the refrigerator for you."

"Thanks," I say.

"Work to live, live to work," she says, sighing.

Upstairs, I go online for news of the volcano. I chew on a nail as I scroll through photos. The smoke and ash are thick and black.

Oh my God, oh my God, I can't do this. Someone who lived near the volcano is missing because he refused to evacuate. I feel dizzy as I grab my purple journal from my desk. I address my entry to my grandmother:

Dear Grandma,

A volcano in Washington erupted, and it's all my fault. The worst part is I don't even really know how it happened. I don't think the earth was even asking for it. I think I maybe tripped and fell onto something that triggered it. How are you not here, helping me figure any of this out? I wake up forgetting you're gone, and then before

I even blink open my eyes, I remember and I just don't want to get out of bed. I know I have to. I know I must continue on. I'm trying, Grandma. I'm wearing your uniform in the hopes that it gives me strength.

Love, Chloe

Chapter Nine

On Sunday, Felix arrives in a blue suit. He looks nicer than I do in my simple black dress.

"Are you okay?" he asks.

I shake my head no.

"Of course you're not," he says. "That was a stupid question that stupid people ask when they don't know what else to say."

"Don't stress," I tell him.

We drive caravan-style on the freeway and then up the curvy mountain roads leading to Kismo. I requested to bring the urn with me in Felix's car, and was surprised that Mom let me. I hold it tightly in my lap, a final hug for the grandmother who gave me so many. Turns out Shannon is in Los Angeles with her family this weekend anyway, so it's only me and Felix in the car.

"Chlo, I'm just worried about you," Felix says. "You've barely said a word this whole time."

"I'm just thinking," I respond.

And it's true. I'm thinking about how to explain the story behind the story here, so Felix can *really* know what's going on. Grandma said not to tell anyone until I turn twenty-one and the job of Mother Nature is officially mine. Well, I'm still not twenty-one, of course, but the job is officially mine. *That's* what I'm thinking about.

Not only did I create the perfect sunny but cool weather for my grandma's funeral, but I added a touch of wind, so that her ashes will truly scatter, not simply land at our feet.

I want to tell all this to Felix, but I keep my mouth shut for now.

It's still warm for October, and purple wildflowers dot the hillsides that my ancestors created. I take in the view with a new curiosity. What on earth am I expected to add to this already perfect landscape?

My ears crackle as we continue our ascent.

"She had a remarkable life," Grandma's friend Pearl says when we've reached our destination. A small crowd of people—some who I recognize, others who I don't—have congregated around the turnout area. "She loved her family. Her friends. And nature," Pearl says, and I wonder if she knows the truth.

Dad's standing apart from the crowd. He blows me a kiss when he sees me.

"I love you, Aunt Fern," my cousin Gerald says, taking some ashes and scattering them in the wind.

"Words fail me," my mom says when it's her turn to speak, and I pray she doesn't go on some endless monologue. My prayers are answered, because that's all she says as she drops a few ashes to the ground. But that's all she has to say about her own mother? Really? I don't think I'll ever understand.

I take a handful of the ashes. They feel like dirt and gravel. I can't stand the fact that this is what's left of my beautiful grandmother, Mother Nature. I think about the ground I'm standing on. If we are all reduced to ashes and dust, then wouldn't that mean that every single one of us is connected to the earth? To her?

"I love you so much, Grandma," I say as I throw the ashes into the air. "I promise I'll make you proud."

I watch Grandma fly back through the universe and wonder how I will ever wash my hands again.

I was all ready to talk to Curtis about poetry in Chorus today. I psyched myself up in bed last night when I couldn't sleep. But for some reason, I can't even look at him now as I make my way to my spot on the bleachers. I'm carrying volcano guilt energy and feeling paranoid, like everyone can tell.

When Ms. Cassidy enters the room she announces, "Today we're going to start our journey with Journey!"

Curtis looks back toward me, but I stare straight ahead, nervous to meet his gaze.

"Show of hands if 'Don't Stop Believin'' rings a bell," she says.

More than half the class raises theirs, as do I. I know it because Dad's cover band played it ad nauseam when I was younger.

"It has a beautiful message, it's a catchy tune, and there's a part for everyone," Ms. Cassidy says, reaching into her bag to extract the sheet music.

When handed the pile, I take a sheet and pass it to the person next to me. I scan the lyrics to the song. That's me, I think, a small-town girl . . .

After class, Curtis is standing in the doorway talking to Ms. Cassidy. I try to squeeze past them, but Curtis puts his foot out, and if I hadn't noticed, I would have tripped over it. "Hold up," he says to me, before finishing his conversation with our teacher.

"It's going to be a dazzling December concert," Ms. Cassidy says to both of us. "I can count on the two of you for the Solstice Sing Along, yes? You know I hate when students call in sick at the last minute."

"Of course," Curtis says. "Wouldn't miss it."

"Me neither," I say. How could I? Chorus is my only A.

Curtis falls in step with me, and we walk down the hall together.

"This is gonna sound so corny," he tells me, "but one of the college applications—I think it's Harvard, actually—asks you to write an essay about how you might change the world or affect the world or something, and I'm writing mine about singing. Out of everything I do, I think singing and being a part of a chorus gives me the most potential to change the world." He laughs. "This coming from a probable poli-sci major."

"Singing's the only time I can turn off my mind and just *be*," I say.

"Exactly!" he says. "You get it!"

I don't tell him this, but sometimes, when we are all in sync, when we all hit the right notes and harmonize, it moves me to tears.

"I saw you at the Harvest Dance," he says. "That was an epic storm."

"Yeah," I say solemnly, thinking about Grandma.

"My date tried to turn the occasion into a rager at her house, but no one showed up."

"So you left?" I say too quickly.

He nods. "I was heading back to school, but the weather was so bad I just went home."

I want to know more about his date. Or do I? He didn't say *girlfriend*.

"So, what are you up to this weekend, Chloe?" he asks.

"Nothing much. Dinner with my dad tonight . . ." *Monitoring the world for the rest of my life.* "What about you?"

"I'm heading to Mount Kismo on Friday after school."

"What are you doing up there?"

"Snowboarding," he says. "Have you ever been?"

"I've been to Kismo, but I've never been snowboarding." I think back to last weekend, scattering Grandma's ashes on the mountain.

"My family has a cabin. I try to go up every weekend in the winter. It's so awesome tearing down the mountain. It's my favorite thing in the world. Next to singing, of course."

"Of course," I say, smiling.

I make a mental note to deliver him more snow.

"Aw, man, you've gotta try it," he says. "Once you get the hang, it's like you're part of the mountain or something."

Well, that's one way of putting it.

"Hey, would you ever want to come up sometime?"

My brain stalls. Did he just invite me to a cabin in the woods?

"Unless you're too busy," he says, filling my silence. "I remember how busy junior year was."

"Oh, um, wow. I—"

"I know you don't drive, but you're welcome to bring a friend. I mean, if you want. No pressure or anything . . ."

"I want to!" I say, a little too enthusiastically. But I need to figure out how to make it work. A day trip wouldn't keep me away from the office for too long.

"Great!" he says. "Gimme your hand," and I stick out my palm. He flips it upside down and writes his number in red ink. "Well, here's my cell," he says. "I have crappy reception up there, but other than that it works."

"What would Brooklyn think about this?" I say, showing him his number on the back of my hand.

"Brooklyn Weber?"

I nod.

"Why?" he says.

"I mean, didn't you . . . Aren't you . . . The Harvest Dance and everything."

"Oh, that night," he says. Then he whispers, "She asked me over a megaphone at lunch. I had to say yes, if you know what I mean."

I smile all the way to my next class.

Dad and I are sitting in a corner booth at the King Road Café. For a short period, I was shuttled to his house every other weekend as a custody tester, but none of us were into it, especially him. He had two girlfriends who didn't know about each other and a bunch of deadbeat friends who played instruments and called themselves a band. I was probably seven at the time, and even I knew they weren't a real band.

Lately, though, we've been trying to have dinner at least once a month. His idea. I told him I was too busy this month with everything going on since Grandma died, but he insisted it wouldn't take too long, and that it was important for consistency in our relationship, or something like that. He knows I've been elevated to my role as Mother Nature sooner than anticipated, and I think he's worried. Or maybe not. I never know with him. I finally agreed when he suggested an early-bird dinner, like old people. At least I could eat and then get back to the office for more monitoring.

"So, how are you doing with everything?" he asks, once the food comes. He bites into his burger, and ketchup drips down his fingers.

"It's a lot," I say. "I just wish she'd trusted Mom with the job."

"I hear you," he says after a long slurp of Dr Pepper. "But Grandma was a smart woman."

Oh, he's doing it again—calling his ex-mother-in-law *Grandma*, a term too sweet for someone who used to refer to him as my *dead-beat dad*.

"Your mother—" he starts. He shakes his head in a memory and then runs his hand over his face.

"What?" I ask.

"Nothing."

He now has ketchup on his cheek. I roll my eyes and motion for him to wipe it off.

"A *privilege*," he says. "You've been bequeathed a privilege. A badge of honor. It's yours, Chloe. Wars are fought over lesser privileges."

I pick at my veggie burger.

"I guess," I say.

"What do you mean you guess? You have to *know* it," he says. "You can't second-guess it. You have to flex a little!"

"How do you know that word?" I ask.

"The gram!" he says proudly.

I hold my hand up in an attempt to stop him from trying any more slang.

"The truth is, your grandmother was a powerful woman. And so are you."

A snort escapes me.

"When Mom and I started going together—"

"No one calls it that," I tell him.

"Sorry . . . *dating*," he clarifies. "We were sophomores in college. Laurel was just so much fun to be around. She had a million friends and was very involved in school and all these activities. I had no idea what she saw in me."

"That's so sad."

"Except maybe that I could keep up with her. We just slipped into things so quickly. Really, I was the luckiest guy on the planet," he says. "She brought me home to meet Grandma during that first summer."

"How was that?"

"Um . . . unforgettable. Your grandmother gave me the stink eye from the second I walked into the house." Dad imitates her by wrinkling his nose. "That's how she looked at me the whole weekend. I told Laurel, 'Your mom hates me,' and she said, 'No, no, you're crazy. You're just misinterpreting.' And then later in the summer, on a picnic, Laurel told me about the whole Mother Nature thing. Naturally, I didn't believe her at first."

"Naturally."

"Um . . . but . . . I came around. How couldn't I? There was proof. The entire setup was in the den of their house at the time. It was incredible. I was even more confounded as to why she was with me at that point," he says. "In the fall, we'd declared our majors and were happily into our junior year when . . . well . . . you were conceived."

"Dad!"

"We were both completely shocked. I mean, beyond shocked."

I don't want to even think about my parents having sex, but the image keeps trying to push its way through. *Aaargh! Make it stop!*

"We were twenty, and your mom was poised to take over her mom's position, as all the Lovejoy women had throughout the centuries—"

"Wait, what? *Mom* was taking over the position?"

Dad nods. "And I was so excited to go on the adventure with

her. We went home in February to tell your grandmother the news, and while we thought she might not be jumping for joy, we certainly didn't think she'd fly into the rage she did."

I cannot picture my grandmother flying into anything, especially a rage.

"She said your mom couldn't manage the task *and* have a baby at the same time. Chloe"—he pauses for a second—"your grandmother was a power-hungry, controlling woman. There. I've said it. I'm expecting the earth to split open and for me to fall in now."

"It won't," I assure him. "But Grandma was so—"

"Deceiving," Dad says. "From you, she wanted your undivided love . . . and you gave it to her. But you're the only one she gave it back to. She would have used any excuse to stay in command."

"This is too much," I say. So, Mom *was* supposed to be Mother Nature?

"You were born in September, and we were so gaga over your cute little face. To be honest, that time is a complete blur. Your grandmother raged. Your mom retreated. I was caring for an infant at age twenty-one. We dropped out of school. What a mess," he says, shaking his head.

I'm not sure how to respond, or how I'm expected to take this all in, this fractured fairy tale of a story. My origin story. I've heard it before, but I never really took it in the way I am now. I reach for the glass of water, but I've already finished it.

"Oh, Chloe," he says.

I am in no mood for apologetic hugs. But I do consider, for the very first time in my life, that maybe, just maybe, this is the reason my mom is the way she is—because she was judged for getting pregnant and then passed over for becoming Mother Nature. And I can't help but feel a twinge of empathy.

I have to try and be nicer to her, I tell myself.

But when Dad says, "You could, yes," I realize I said it out loud.

Dad drops me off at home, and before I get out of the car we make plans for our November dinner next month.

I head back to the office to check in on things, but I'm distracted by a shadowy figure sitting at the side of the swimming pool. It startles me at first, but as I get closer, I see it is my mom—a glass of wine in one hand, *The Book of Nature* in the other.

Shit. Why is it out here? How did she get into the office? The key is still hanging around my neck.

"What are you doing?" I ask calmly as I approach.

"I'm Mother Nature," she says, in an unusually deep voice.

I notice an almost-empty wine bottle next to her. "Mom—"

"No, seriously, look at me. I'm Mother Nature. The way things should have been." She blows air through her lips, mimicking the wind. She lifts the wineglass in her hand. "Oh no!" she says. "Earthquake." And she starts shaking it.

"All right, let's get you up to bed," I suggest, as I have a million times before.

I lean down to reach for her, but she shrugs me away.

"What are you doing? C'mon, Mom!"

"Don't 'C'mon, Mom' me, young lady. I'm Mother Nature," she says, fluttering her feet in the water, splashing it everywhere, even on *The Book of Nature*. "Tidal wave!"

"Mother, don't!" I say, insistent.

"Look. Tidal waaaave!" She kicks her feet harder.

“Where did you get that?” I say, reaching out to grab *The Book of Nature* from her. But she pulls back hard.

And then, in slow motion, it’s opening midair—like some majestic bird—before landing with a splash and sinking to the bottom of the pool.

Chapter Ten

I see what's happened, but my brain can't make sense of it. Why would she do this to me? It's the wine—too much wine. I look to my mother for some sort of explanation or apology. I look to her for a solution to this problem she caused. She is lit only by moonlight, and she looks smug and satisfied, but I don't want to believe it; this can't be right.

Despite being fully dressed, I dive into the cold water and swim to the bottom of the pool. The book is sitting on top of the drain, ink bleeding off its pages in ribbons. I grab it, but when I do, a few pages come loose from the binding and float out of my grasp.

I burst to the surface, the soggy, ruined book clutched to my chest, ready to confront my mom, only there is nothing but an empty wine bottle at the edge of the pool. When I hoist myself out, I notice that Curtis's phone number has washed off my hand. This must be some sort of cosmic joke, only it isn't funny at all.

I'm shaking now, and not just because it's cold. "Mother!" I yell into the night.

Only the sound of a distant dog barking returns my call.

"*Mo*ther!" I yell again as I head into the house, dripping wet.

I find her in the kitchen, doing dishes. "*I'm* Mother Nature," I scream at her.

"You're just a child," she sneers, glaring at me. "Go get a towel and wipe up this floor right now."

She leans against the kitchen counter, drinking her wine. There is nothing else to say to her, nothing she will ever hear, so I turn around and stomp out of the kitchen, trying not to let her see me cry, tracking pool water all the way to the sliding back door.

In the office, I inspect *The Book of Nature*. It's soggy and congealed, pages clumping together, some blank, some smudged, others missing. I set it down on the floor and collapse into the wheely chair, my face glazed in tears. Grandma never would have let this happen under her watch.

The lights blink, the Earth hologram pulsates, the heartbeat of the world thumps in my own backyard, but I have no idea how to tend to any of it. I glance up at the little black intercom on a shelf, and I remember Grandma saying something about someone I could contact in an emergency. And if this isn't an emergency, I don't know what is.

I bring the intercom down to my level, hoping this won't set off some sort of new global catastrophe.

"Hello, hello?" I say into it, but there's no answer.

Then I notice an ON/OFF button that seems off. I'm afraid to push it, but I don't think there's an alternative at this point. Quickly, I press my finger to it, and a little indicator light blinks green.

"Hello, hello?" I say again. "This is an emergency. This is Chloe Lovejoy. Fern Lovejoy's granddaughter. Is anyone there?" I listen intently for a response, and I think I hear the faint crackle of static. I start tapping my foot in anticipation. "Hello? I was told I could contact someone in an emergency. Is anyone there?"

"Yes, hello?" I finally hear from the speaker—a man's voice. "This is Chloe?"

"No, *this* is Chloe," I respond.

"Yes," the voice says. "I'm just confirming that it's Chloe who I'm speaking to."

"Yes, yes," I say. "My grandmother died and . . . and . . . and I'm now Mother Nature?"

"I know," the voice says solemnly. "And please let me extend my condolences. Your grandmother was a wonderful woman. A wonderful Mother Nature."

"Thank you," I say. "Who is this?"

"Sorry!" he says. "This is Wade. Didn't she tell you about me?"

"Hi, Wade. Yes, she mentioned that I could contact you in an emergency." I gaze at the saturated book next to me. I'm in big trouble—I know it—but I have to tell him. The world is at stake.

"You probably didn't notice me," he says, "but I was at your grandmother's funeral. I should have introduced myself, but it just didn't seem like the right time."

I close my eyes and try to picture a face that might match this voice, but everything that day was a blur, as it is right now. And his voice is sort of nondescript, so I imagine he is, too.

"Thank you for being there," I say. I've calmed down a little, now that there's somebody to talk to.

"Of course," he says. "Your grandmother was very special. Our families have been aligned since the beginning of time, so I wouldn't have missed the opportunity to say goodbye to her."

"Oh, so you inherited your position, too?"

"Yes," he says. "My father passed five years ago, and that's when I stepped in."

"I'm so sorry," I say.

"Thank you. It's been a pleasure serving your grandmother. I was reluctant to do this job at first, as you can imagine. It's a lot, but it's been my honor."

"Wade," I say. "I've got a big problem." I don't know how to tell him that my drunk mother destroyed centuries of history by waving *The Book of Nature* around next to the pool. But I have to.

"Go on," he says.

"*The Book of Nature* is ruined," I say quickly.

"Is what?"

"Is *ruined*," I say into the intercom, bursting into tears. "There was an accident, and it ended up at the bottom of our pool."

"Oh my," he says. "It was removed from the office?"

"I'm so sorry," I say, and I know it sounds like *I* ruined it, but I just don't have the capacity or the energy to explain.

"Chloe, calm down, please," he says. "You're saying the book is at the bottom of the pool?"

"No, I dove in and grabbed it. But it's useless now, and I only got to read a few chapters fully before this happened," I confess. "It's right here next to me, but the pages are all—"

I hear him sigh. "Listen," he says. "You're going to have to come see me."

"Now?"

"In the next twenty-four hours. I'll give you directions. I'm deep on Mount Kismo."

"Kismo?"

"Yes, not that far from where your grandmother's ashes are scattered," he says.

"But I don't have a car."

"You'll need one to get here," he says curtly.

"Can I bring a friend? Or rather, can a friend bring me?"

He sighs again. "Others aren't supposed to know yet. Not until you're twenty-one. But these are extenuating circumstances, so . . . whatever it takes."

I imagine I'll have to get Felix or Shannon to bring me, but how or what am I going to tell them?

"You have another book there?" I say, relieved.

Wade chortles. "No, Chloe, unfortunately that is the original *Book of Nature*, handed down through the ages. But fortunately, we just finished digitizing it. I'm going to try to put it on a portable device, which I'll give to you. It's all I can think to do right now," he says. "You have to understand—in all of history, this has never happened before."

Of course it hasn't. Leave it to me. Leave it to my mother.

"What's the address?" I ask, reaching for a pen and paper.

"The directions are complicated," he says.

"That's okay, I'll use GPS."

"Chloe," he says. "It's not GPS-able. I'm going to have to scan them for you."

"Okay," I say. "But where will I get them?"

"The main terminal," he says.

I don't know what he's talking about.

"The computer next to the cloud board?"

"No, no," he says. "The main one. The giant one. You're probably standing right over it now."

But, no, I'm standing in front of a giant desk— Oh! It's not a desk. It's a computer, the screen right in front of my face.

"I see," I say, and he explains how to retrieve it.

The office is pinging and pulsing and popping, and I think I'm starting to panic because I'm trembling—freezing from the pool water, of course, and shaking from everything else that has gone down tonight.

"When should I expect you, Chloe?" Wade asks, and before I can answer he adds, "As soon as possible, I hope?"

"Yes, yes," I say, picturing the steep road up to Kismo, wondering about my English quiz, the paper due for History, the ACT I have yet to sign up for. "Is there anything I should do tonight in here?" I ask, looking around.

"Set *The Book of Nature* out under the lamp by the rainbow boards," Wade says, "and keep that lamp on all night and all day. Turn the pages daily to help the drying process. Let me know if anything restores." He says that I can leave everything else as is until after we meet. "It isn't ideal," he adds. "But it will have to do."

“Okay,” I say. “I promise I’ll do it.”

I can’t deal with seeing Mom, plus I need to keep an eye on everything here, so I push two chairs together in the office as a makeshift bed, and try to fall asleep amidst the blinking, twinkling world.

Chapter Eleven

The next morning, I don't even grab breakfast and I don't say hi or bye to my mom. I bike to school as fast as I can, a flock of birds following above, and grab Felix just as he's stepping into his English class. "Emergency," I say, and without question he turns around and follows me down the hallway. "Do you know where Shannon is?"

"She has her meeting with Mrs. Boyle," he says. "What's wrong? You look like shit. Where are we going?"

"Your car," I say.

"Oh, this is serious."

"You have no idea."

And while students file into their classrooms, Felix and I make our way out to to the parking lot until we find his silver Prius. "I need to go to Kismo," I say, digging into my backpack for a copy of the instructions Wade sent me last night.

"Mount Kismo? Right this second?"

I nod.

"Three o'clock's too late?"

"It is."

"Because . . ."

I take in a deep breath and let it out slowly. "Because . . ." The car feels stuffy. I crack the window. "Because my mother did something last night."

"Like what?" Felix says, concerned.

"This was a bad one. Maybe the worst ever. Can you start the car, please?"

"I still don't understand why we're going all the way to Kismo. Do you have to see her sponsor or something?"

"Her sponsor? Are you kidding me? She's not in AA! She's just an A. In her rage, she threw *The Book of Nature* into the pool, and it's completely ruined, and—"

"Whoa, whoa," he says. "What the hell's *The Book of Nature*?"

"Well," I start. Then I think, *I just have to say it—I have to release the words.* I know Grandma said to keep it on the down-low, but these are extenuating circumstances, as Wade confirmed.

I take another deep breath, and I exhale, but I can't bring myself to do it. Instead, I extract the sheet of paper from my backpack and hand it to him.

"'Take a right at the fourth turnout, and park and walk through the canopy of leaves until you reach a brook'? C'mon, what is this, Chloe?"

"Directions to Wade's cabin," I say. "Can you please start the car?"

I close my eyes, and we sit in silence until I hear the motor turn. When I open them, we're finally heading out of the parking lot.

"This better not be someone you met on Bumble," he warns.

"What? Of course not." And then I add, "I'm not on Bumble!"

"Whatever's going on," Felix says in a flat but concerned voice, "you owe me one. My parents will kill me when they find out I'm not in English, or French, or History."

"Anything and everything," I promise. "I owe you the world."

The silence between us is incredibly awkward, and I can't tell if he's irritated or mad, or just plain scared, so I reach over and turn on the radio. "Emotional Rescue" blasts from the speakers—the Rolling Stones. I crank the volume up even higher and keep it that way for the next hour.

Wade is short, dressed in green khakis and a white button-down shirt. He's got a thick head of brown hair. From afar, he looks like he's my dad's age. But as we approach, his face looks young—really young. More like my age, if that's even possible.

"You made it," he says, his voice slightly nasal.

"This is my friend Felix," I tell him.

"A pleasure," Wade says, extending his hand, but Felix doesn't take it. Instead, I step in and shake it. His hands are soft and small.

"Come," Wade says, and we enter the small cabin—which looks nothing like the office back at my house. It's just a regular cabin in the woods. Wade leads us to the kitchen. "Can I make you some tea?" he asks.

I say, "Yes, please," as Felix says, "No, thanks."

We sit at the round kitchen table while Wade puts on the kettle. "I'm going to grab the device from out back," he says, and leaves us alone there.

"What are we doing?" Felix whispers. "Is this a d-r-u-g situation?"

"I told you, *The Book of Nature* drowned in the pool. I'll explain everything—"

"This is so sus. It's Wednesday morning, and I'm at some *weirdo's* cabin all the way on Kismo, and you can't even tell me why?"

"Y'know," I say, "you are totally stressing me out."

"I'm stressing *you* out?"

Felix looks exasperated. I have to tell him now. I take a deep inhale, and on the exhale . . . nothing comes out but breath. I take another, deeper inhale and say, "My grandmother gave me this on my birthday." I show him the key around my neck.

"Yes," he says. "I remember. You thought you were getting a car."

"And this key unlocks the door to Mother Nature's headquarters," I say, trying to gauge his reaction, "which is in our backyard."

He's never going to believe me, but there—I did it. I. Did. It.

"Naturally," Felix says.

"I was supposed to be in training for the next five years, but remember the storm the night of the dance?"

He doesn't even nod. He just stares at me, impatient, annoyed.

"That was my grandmother, *the* Mother Nature, having a *stroke* at the control panel. I mean, she was purposely making it blustery at first—as a favor to me—but then she had the stroke. And that's why things got so out of control. Don't you remember that night? The rain, the sleet, the snow?"

Felix averts his eyes.

"I'm not even supposed to be telling you any of this," I say. "And now she's dead, and I'm Mother Nature, and to make a long, long, long story short, my mom . . . my mom . . . Uch, anyway, *The Book of Nature*—like the Bible of how to do my job—ended up in the pool, and it's *ruined*. And we're here now to figure this out."

The kettle screams, and Felix jumps a little. "I think you need help, Chlo."

I stand up to turn off the stove. "I do need help. That's why we're here."

"Not that kind of h—"

"Chloe, can you come back here?" Wade suddenly calls out.

Felix stands. "You're not going anywhere," he says. "You need a psychiatrist."

I push past him. "Stop it. You're so untrusting. Come with me." I reach for his hand, but I end up with his wrist, and I pull him out of the chair and down the hallway to a sliding door. Wade is motioning to me from a shed on the other side.

"You have to see something," he says, and I sense an urgency in his voice.

As I tug Felix toward the shed, I notice that it's a smaller version of the converted garage—my office—with banks of levers and blinking lights, graphs and maps and buttons lining the walls.

“What is all this?” Felix asks cautiously.

“I told you,” I say.

“Come in,” Wade says, leading us inside.

“Chloe!” Felix says.

“I know,” I say, moving from his wrist to his hand.

Wade leads us to a mounted screen at the far end of the room, and when we gather around it, we see a grainy black-and-white image of Mom jimmying open the office window last night in our backyard.

“Oh my God!” I say. I knew she must have figured out a way in there in order to get the book in the first place, but I didn’t know she’d look like some cat burglar.

“She broke in,” Wade says. “And I’m sorry to say, but I don’t trust that she won’t do it again. I don’t trust your mother, and you shouldn’t, either.”

“Oh, don’t worry,” I say. “I don’t.”

Felix’s phone rings, and he gives me an imploring look before taking it out of his pocket. “It’s Shannon,” he announces in a panicked tone. “What am I supposed to tell her?”

Wade looks over. “You get service up here?”

“Let it go to voicemail,” I tell Felix. “Please.”

Felix clicks a button and sighs.

Wade unplugs what looks like a black hard drive from an outlet below the television monitor and shows it to me. It’s so simple, a shiny, black device that fits in the palm of my hand. “Your grandmother was very skeptical about this new technology,” he says. “As every generation is, I suppose.”

Felix clears his throat.

"Wait, this little thing contains the entire *Book of Nature*?" I ask, and Wade gives it to me.

"Not only that," Wade says, "but we're working on the technology that's currently operating in the office. Soon you'll be able to utilize this device for everything."

I flip it over in my hands. "How is that even possible?"

Wade explains that a team has been working on the technology for decades. That it's imperfect at this stage but it's getting closer every day. He presses a button and a small screen lights up. He punches in a code and scrolls through some text before showing me. "See? Here you can adjust the font size if it's too small."

"So it's like a Kindle?" Felix says.

Wade and I both look at him.

"No," Wade says. "It's very much not like a Kindle."

"Felix is one of my best friends since forever," I say. "I literally just told him about all this in your kitchen less than a minute ago."

"Understood," Wade says. "I guess skepticism is natural for everyone."

"So, I'm supposed to believe that this is Mother Nature's headquarters?" Felix asks.

"Well, no," I say. "HQ is in *my* backyard."

"This is more like tech support," Wade explains.

"So Chloe's the Steve Jobs," Felix says sarcastically. "And you're the Genius Bar?"

"I don't know what that is," Wade says.

"This is the Apple store," I tell Felix, pointing to the shed, "and he's the genius."

Wade smiles politely.

Felix gives me an urgent look.

"What are we going to do about your mother?" Wade asks me, and I hope it's a hypothetical question and he's not expecting me to answer, because I've *never* known what to do about my mother. "I sent contractors over there this morning," he says.

"To my house?"

Wade nods. "They replaced the window and installed an alarm and changed the lock."

"Oh no," I say, holding the key. I promised Grandma I'd never give it up.

"Don't worry," Wade says. "New lock, same key." I don't even know what that means.

"I didn't see anyone at the house this morning," I say.

"No, you were probably still sleeping," he explains. "They arrived early, as usual."

"You mean they've been there before?"

"For decades," Wade says.

I'd assumed all those people I saw coming in and out of the garage throughout the years were the gardeners and the pool guy.

Eventually, the three of us head back to the kitchen in the main cabin, where we sit around the table and Wade pours us each a mug of peppermint tea—tepid now, since we were gone for so long. Felix keeps looking from me to Wade, like he's waiting for one of us to break the charade.

Wade schools me on the intricacies of the device. This time, I record him on my iPhone, to catch every single detail, every word he utters, every nuance. I'm to read the entirety of *The Book of Nature*—that's the priority, he instructs. I can barely keep up with the reading in my English class, but somehow I'll have to persevere.

"Be careful," he says as he officially hands the device to me. "Keep it with you at all times, and contact me when you need me. Nothing's too big or too small," he says. "I promise."

"I promise, too," I say, clutching it in my hand.

Felix raises his hand to wave goodbye, but he still refuses to shake.

As Felix negotiates his way out of the dirt driveway, he looks over at me, eyes wide, skin a little pale.

"I know," I say.

"You know what?"

"I know how freaked out you are."

"I don't think you do," he says.

"I felt the same way. I thought my grandma had dementia, remember?"

"It's . . . I'm . . . You're . . ."

"Just don't bother," I say. "There are no words. I know."

Felix attaches his phone to his car and quickly dials a number.

"Who are you ca—" I start.

But before I can finish asking my question, Shannon's voice says, "Hello?"

Chapter Twelve

I don't go home. I just had the most awkward conversation with Shannon, who pretty much stayed silent the whole time I talked. Plus, I have no desire to see my mother. Instead, I have Felix drop me off at the park, the one I used to play at as a kid. "You okay?" I ask before I exit his car.

"Um . . ."

"I don't want it to get weird between us."

"No, no," he says, but already I can tell it is.

"Shannon was so quiet," I say. "It's like she didn't believe me."

He shrugs. "Can you really blame her?"

As Felix drives away, I can see him looking at me through the rearview mirror.

I head over to the swings. The park is nearly empty except for a mom and her two sons, who are playing by the slides. When I was little, I would escape here, to the swings, when I couldn't deal with what was happening with my mother at home, her bad boyfriends, her fights with her mom.

I sit on a swing and pump my legs, gaining momentum, and soon I'm flying through the air, back and forth, back and forth, the wind from the motion blowing my hair out of my face, the rhythm calming me down.

It's a beautiful day, and Morro Rock shines in the distance. I used to come here with Grandma, and she'd sit on the grass—not on the benches where all the other grown-ups sat. Sometimes we'd have a picnic. I'd freak out if any ants or flies or bees invaded, which they often did, but Grandma would always soothe my fears by telling me how beautiful the creatures were. She'd say not to be afraid—that they were only coming to investigate our world before returning to theirs.

About half an hour later, I'm done replaying memories and the events of the day, so I push myself off the swing and land with bent knees in the gravel—the perfect dismount. Then I grab my backpack and find a patch of grass and lie there, letting the late afternoon sun beat down on my face as it sets through the clouds.

I keep picturing Felix's expression when I told him I was Mother Nature—full of bewilderment, awe, and fear.

I close my eyes and listen to the hum of insects as they whiz past me. I'm too tired to even swat them away. Up in the trees, birds sing to one another. One croaks out a four-part tune, while another answers in a high-pitched chirp. I open one eye, and find a white butterfly winging around my shoes. When I wiggle my foot, it moves toward my stomach, circling low and close but never landing.

My eyes are starting to close again, and although I try to stay awake, I succumb to sleep. Soon, I'm sitting on Grandma's bed back at the house, and she's braiding my hair, but she's tugging too hard, and when I ask her to stop, it's Brooklyn who's behind me pulling my hair.

I awake with a start, and the first thing I see is that I'm being swarmed by butterflies—white, pale yellow, red speckled—fluttering their frenzied wings all around me. I force myself to stay still. I've never seen a butterfly from this perspective, let alone thirty, forty, or fifty of them. What do they want? Or are they responding to me, giving me permission to accept my fate?

A woman approaches. "I wish I had my phone with me," she says, barely above a whisper. "It's beautiful."

When I finally get home, I let myself into the house, unsure if Mom's even there, and immediately go back to the office. I charge the little black device and take a walk around the spinning-Earth hologram. Then I sit in Grandma's wheely chair, find the remote, and turn on the Weather Channel.

The anchor is doing a piece on the dwindling puffin population in Iceland. I make a note to research this. The next story is about deforestation in Oregon, which is really a story about people getting in the way of Mother Nature—rather, of me. Again.

* * *

The next day, I'm late to English because I've been crouching in the bathroom stall trying to monitor the earth from the little black device.

"Good morning," Mr. Rosenberg says as I make my way to my seat. "Did you ride over to this land by boat with your father?"

I have no idea what he's talking about.

"Who can tell me what play that's from? I'll give you a hint: It's not a comedy."

No one answers. I take my seat.

"I'll give you another hint: They ride over in a huge storm," he says. "A huge storm," he says louder. "What's another word for 'a huge storm'?"

"Monsoon," someone calls out.

I turn around. "That's specifically a wind," I say.

"Thank you, Ms. Duncan Sunshine," Mr. Rosenberg says.

The class laughs, and I sink deeper into my seat.

"Did Shakespeare write a play called *The Monsoon*?" he asks.

Again, no one answers.

"*The Tempest*!" he says, all riled up. "Prospero, Miranda . . . If anything, you should know that word for the ACT. 'Tempest' is another word for 'storm.'"

So is squall *or* blizzard*, or* hurricane, I want to say, but I don't want to be rude. I dig into my backpack for *The Comedy of Errors*, but unfortunately I seem to have left it at home again.

Mr. Rosenberg keeps me after class. "Ms. Lovejoy," he says, motioning with his long index finger for me to come to his desk.

When I approach, he tilts his head to the side. "How come you missed the quiz yesterday?"

"I was sick," I say quickly.

He places his hands across his chest.

"Is there something going on at home that you'd like to talk about?"

"Definitely not," I say.

Mr. Rosenberg looks at me suspiciously. "Chloe, I'm sure you don't need me to remind you that this is your junior year, essentially your last chance to show colleges what you're made of. Missing your English quiz isn't going to impress anyone."

"I know," I say, looking down toward my shoes.

We stay like this, in silence for a few uncomfortable seconds.

"Can I still take it?" I ask. I bite my lower lip, then force a smile.

He narrows his eyes. "Of course not. How do I know someone hasn't told you all the answers?"

"Nobody's told me anything," I say. It's the story of my life.

I'm about to skulk out the door when I take a chance and ask, "Are you offering any sort of extra credit?"

"Well," he says cautiously. "I suppose that's something we can talk about."

In Spanish, I sit toward the back of class and sneak in more of my required *Book of Nature*, reading from the device while the rest of the students conjugate verbs. Patience is one of the traits required for Mother Nature, and unfortunately patience is one of many things I lack.

"¿Usted entiende, señorita?" the teacher says about a complicated verb. "Chloe?"

Do you understand?

"Sí," I say. When what I really mean is no.

* * *

I climb the bleachers in Chorus, saying hello—like, a normal hello—to Curtis on the way up. I don't fumble with small talk. I don't lose my train of thought. He smiles and mouths, *Hi.*

Ms. Cassidy hits a note on the piano, and we begin singing "Don't Stop Believin'."

Felix finds me at my locker and practically drags me down the hallway. "She thinks we're making it up," he says, and I know he means Shannon. There is a bench a few feet away on the sidewalk in front of school. We notice it at the same time. "I'm texting her to meet us here," he says.

Cars drive by. Birds tweet. The city bus pulls over, thinking we're boarding, but we wave it away. "Can't we do this later?" I beg Felix, but Shannon finally arrives and sits down with us.

"You guys are such assholes," she says.

"Assholes?" Felix says.

"You're Mother Nature," she says to me. And then to Felix, "And what, you're Father Time?"

He looks my way. "Can you just do a demonstration or something?" he begs. "To prove it to her?"

I'm pretty sure I'm not supposed to be so public about it, but I reach in my bag for the device and turn it on. It's currently sunny and cloudless, but I navigate to the rainbow coordinates. I can still see Shannon's expression out of the corner of my eye. It reads, *Don't mess with me*. I swipe a rainbow.

"Look behind you," I suggest.

When she does, she says, "Gorgeous rainbow," but it's clear she's unconvinced. She doesn't even acknowledge that it's not raining.

"Chloe," Felix starts.

"I'm trying!"

"Make it rain," he says.

"No," I say. "I'll make it snow."

"You're scaring me," Shannon says. "I have to get to class."

She begins to stand up, just as I navigate to snow. Perfect chunky white flakes fall from the sky.

Desperate times, desperate measures, I think.

"Whoa," Felix says.

Shannon looks up, and then toward me, and then up again. "What the—"

Nevertheless, she sticks out her tongue to catch one in her mouth.

"Believe me now?" I ask, before readjusting the device to revert to the sunny day it was. The flakes immediately melt away.

Shannon's still looking up.

"This is between the three of us," I say.

Shannon grabs Felix, her eyes so wide I think they'll explode.

"I know, right?" he says, grabbing her back.

"I can't even tell my grandma?" Shannon says. "She'll never remember."

"Just us," I say as I hold out my hand to shake theirs in agreement.

On my bike ride home, I catch a blur of something, and when I turn, I see a bunch of squirrels running alongside me. Dozens of them, following me down the street. "Shoo!" I tell them. "Please. Get out of the street. You'll get hit!"

And like they understand English, they move over to the sidewalk.

To my left, a herd of cats is meowing near the woods, and above me, a flock of ducks is forming a V in the sky.

"Yes," I tell them all. "It's me, and I'm trying. I'm really trying to be good at this job."

Mom knocks on my bedroom door and opens it at the same time.

"Come in," I say, even though she's already got one foot in the room.

She crosses her arms in front of her chest. "I'm sorry."

It's been days since she tossed *The Book of Nature* into the pool. Could she be apologizing for that? Or is there something new?

"All these feeling were bubbling up, and I took them out on you."

I nod, indicating that I'm listening.

"It was wrong, and I just want you to know it will never happen again."

She waits a few seconds before pivoting and heading out the door.

"Mom!" I call.

"It's okay," she says. "You don't have to say anything."

"Mother!" I call. "Please come back."

Reluctantly, she turns and reenters my room. She walks straight to the foot of my bed and sits. She doesn't say anything at first, just looks around at my stuff.

"What feelings were bubbling up?" I ask.

"You know that saying 'raised by wolves'?"

I nod.

She raises her hand. "That's me. Grandma was always physically around, but she was never *here*—like, the way a kid needs her mom."

Do I tell her that I know exactly what she means? Or is it possible she'll figure it out on her own?

"When I was old enough to understand what was going on, I must have forgiven her on some level, because that's all *I* wanted to be. Mother Nature—just like her. That was gonna be the glue between us. That's when the real bond would start. And at sixteen, we went to Kismo, to a clearing deep in the woods. I swear, it was like *Bambi*. There were deer and rabbits, and it was so charming and thrilling. And she gave me the key . . ."

I'm picturing her story like a movie on the big screen. Dappled light coming in through the trees, soft green grass under everyone's feet, Thumper hopping by.

"I had four years of training, on and off, mostly because I wanted to go to college. I loved getting to finally spend quality time with her—just the two of us. It was like making up for lost time. But when I got pregnant with you it was all just suddenly off the table. The door was shut. More like *slammed* in my face. Done. Over."

This matches what Dad told me, but I still can't picture my sweet grandmother acting this way.

"I'm trying really, really hard not to be . . ."

"Jealous?" I say.

"Bitter," she says. "No one likes a bitter person. Listen, fates are sealed, blah blah blah. I had a moment by the pool, and I promise it will never happen again." She stands up from my bed and walks toward me, I assume to hug me.

But instead, she reaches past me. "It's so stuffy in here," she says, throwing open my window.

Chapter Thirteen

In Chemistry, I see the large hand first—hair on the knuckles, nails a little too long. The hand is on my device, which is on the lab desk. When I turn around, I see Mr. Kortege, his stern expression staring me down.

"It's not a phone," I say, certain this will clear up any misunderstanding.

In one swift move, he sweeps up the device and marches back to his desk, where he throws it into a drawer and slams it shut.

"No, no, no," I say, following him. "I need that."

"You're all addicted to your iPhones," he says, guarding the drawer.

"It's not an iPhone," I say.

"Fine," he says. "Your *Androids*. Go back to your lab partner," he says. "It'll be here when you're done."

"You don't understand," I start, but I'm not quite sure how to explain.

"*You* don't understand," he says forcefully.

The other kids look our way. I can't blame them—I'd do the same—but I don't like the feeling of so many eyes on me.

"I need to see one thing," I say in a whisper.

"Yes, you need to see if your beaker reacted to the protein," he says, pointing to my empty stool.

I think about Wade trusting me with the device. He was worried about food spilling on it or my backpack getting stolen or something like that. I doubt he ever worried about a teacher confiscating it. Or maybe he did. All I know is that I'm letting Wade down. And my grandmother. And her mother. I am a Lovejoy failure.

Mr. Kortege is still pointing, and I'm still standing there, looking like some zombie who can't function without her phone. But he's got it all wrong. I'm Mother Freakin' Nature, for God's sake.

"I need my device," I say, my voice booming in a way I imagine someone with power might speak.

Every single person in our class stops what they're doing and looks at me. "The fate of the world rests in there," I say, pointing to the closed drawer. "Do you understand?"

I hear nervous laughter from my classmates.

"Chloe," Mr. Kortege says, but that's all he says. I see him push a red button next to the chalkboard. He nods and returns his gaze to me.

"Give. It. Back," I snap.

"Return to your experiments," he says nervously to the other kids.

"No, you guys," I say. "I need witnesses to what's going on here."

I know I have no right to do what I'm about to, but out of anger, disrespect, and stress, I yell, "You think I'm argon, don't you? You think I'm lazy and inert. Well, I'm not, Bob Kortege."

Everyone in class is laughing, even Arsenic.

"I'm a fighter," I say. "And I will get that device back!"

He tilts his head back, as though I have bad breath, and his lips curl into an exaggerated grimace. It might all be worth it just for that look on his face.

He's still not opening the drawer, though. What will it take? I hear the *click* of the classroom door opening, and when I turn around, I see a campus security officer, followed by Mrs. Otsawa, the principal.

"Chloe?" she says sternly. "Can you come with me?"

Sure, I can go with her, as long as Bob Kortege returns the device that runs the world.

"Yes, but I need—"

"You'll get," she says. "Now come with me."

Mrs. Otsawa puts me in a chair in the waiting room and steps into her office, shutting the door. All I can think is *Wade's going to kill me, Wade's going to kill me*. After what seems like twenty minutes, she emerges.

"We can't get ahold of your mother," she says.

"She just started a new job," I explain.

"But your father's on his way."

"Why?" I say.

"Chloe, this outburst is very concerning."

"I need that device back," I say.

"Chloe, you're obsessing."

When my dad appears, it feels like another one of my nightmares. He looks so small and confused. There's no way he's going to help my situation. In fact, I'm worried he's going to make it worse. Not that my mom would have made it any better.

"Hey," he says, waving to Mrs. Otsawa like she's a member of his band.

"Mr. Lovejoy?" she says, even though that's not his last name—it's my mother's. "I'm Mrs. Otsawa." They shake hands.

"Hey, Chlo," he says to me.

I give him a thumbs-up.

"I'm worried about Chloe," Mrs. Otsawa says after we're all seated in her office. "She's exhibiting behavior very atypical for her."

Does she not realize I'm sitting right here? "Dad," I say. "I'm fine."

"Chloe, you seem like a reasonable girl," Mrs. Otsawa says. "You have no blemishes on your record up until now. You've always flown under the radar. You must understand why I'm concerned, yes? Why I called your dad here today?"

"Because you couldn't find my mom," I say.

Mrs. Otsawa looks exasperated, and how can I blame her?

"Electronics are absolutely prohibited during class time. And, as it was told to me, Chloe was putting up a fight with her Chemistry teacher when he took her phone."

"It's not a phone," I say, frustrated.

"Whatever it was," Mrs. Otsawa says in a slow, calculated way, "Chloe was inappropriate in her behavior toward her teacher. Neither he, nor I, will tolerate that."

There is a knock on the door, and Mrs. Otsawa stands up. My dad looks at me and reaches over to touch my arm, but I pull away. He shrugs and gives a hangdog look. When Mrs. Otsawa returns to her chair, she's holding my device—thank God.

"That's definitely not a phone," my dad says, looking at it in her hands. "It looks like a hard drive."

I don't think he knows about all the digital conversions that are taking place within the Maparium, and I'm not sure I can convey that to him with only a look. Still, I try. I tilt my head and widen my eyes, leaning forward for emphasis. Much to my surprise, he tilts his head back and nods. I am so grateful for the unspoken understanding. I suppose it makes sense. We are, after all, genetically linked.

"Can I see it?" he asks gently, and Mrs. Otsawa hands it over to him. I am relieved it is now in somewhat safe hands. My dad clears his throat. "Chloe's grandmother passed recently," he says, slipping the device to me.

I click on it and sneakily navigate quickly through the windows, keeping the device low and out of her sight.

"Yes, she told me. My condolences to both of you."

"They were very close," he continues.

I nod in agreement.

"I mean, is it possible that a loss such as this can cause behavioral problems?" he asks.

"Certainly," she says. "Perhaps you would like to talk to a professional about your feelings around the loss." She turns to me. "I can refer you to a number of therapists in the area. Most take insurance," she says, moving to my dad. "If finances are a problem, you can see one who works for the state."

"What do you say, Chlo?" my dad says.

I can't tell if we're putting on an act here, or if he really wants me to speak to a shrink.

"What's the worst that can happen?" he says. "You can vent about us in a safe environment."

Mrs. Otsawa is nodding and smiling.

"I just don't know how it would work, time-wise," I say, stalling.

"It's one hour a week," Mrs. Otsawa says. "Not even an hour. More like fifty minutes."

"Forty, if we're being honest," my dad says, also nodding and smiling.

I can't stand looking at these bobbleheads anymore. "Fine," I say. "Fine."

Chapter Fourteen

"I don't really have to go to therapy, do I?" I ask while we're walking to his car.

"Not unless you want to," he says.

"What would I possibly tell a therapist? That I'm Mother Nature? They'd have me committed. You have no idea what this is like, trying to juggle all of this."

"It's true," he says. "I don't. But can I say something? I think it's time to step into your power. If not now, when?"

In the sixteen years I've known my father, this may be the smartest thing he's ever said. Like, ever.

"I guess," I say.

"No 'guessing.' You have to know it. Like, really, deeply know it." He touches his heart with one hand and his temple with the pointer finger of his other hand.

Mrs. Otsawa told me I'll have to apologize to Mr. Kortege, but she also said I could take the rest of the day off, so I head downtown on my bike after saying goodbye to Dad in the parking lot. My dad's right, though—what I've been bequeathed is a *privilege*. I need an attitude adjustment.

At a vintage store on Morro Bay Boulevard, I comb through racks of clothing I'd normally never wear. But I'm not me anymore—at least not the me that I used to be. *In today's performance, Chloe Lovejoy will be playing the role of Mother Nature.*

I try on a blue dress with a daisy pattern. Then a white skirt with orange outlines of petals, and a black jacket with embroidered leaves. I sift through jewelry at the counter and pick out silver leaf earrings. I grab anything with a flower pattern on it, and if it fits, I add it to my to-buy pile. I find a bag that's made of bright-green fake grass and add it to my loot.

I pay for my haul, and while the salesperson is bagging it, she says, "You're Mother Nature, right?"

This stops me cold.

"For Halloween," she adds. "That's so fun!"

"Ha-Halloween," I stutter, only now realizing why there were so many sexy witches walking down the halls today. "It's tonight?"

She looks at me funny. "Tomorrow, silly!"

"Right!" I say, pretending I was kidding.

My tote bag bulging with a fancy, flowery wardrobe, I bike to a market on the way home and pick up a bag of candy to give out tomorrow. Grandma used to take me trick-or-treating when I was little, and now I'm remembering there were cats—always cats—following us. One year, I was Little Red and she was the Wolf. Another time, she was a flower and I was a bee.

When I'm finally home, I bring the candy into the office and start unwrapping chocolates while reading from *The Book of Nature*. In the chapter on water, I learn that there is the same amount of water on Earth now as there was when Earth formed, which kind of blows my mind. And 97 percent of the world's water is undrinkable! How can that be? I think about the sprinklers on the quad at school, and how they randomly go off at all hours—watering the grass, drenching the students, wasting so much water. I grab a calculator and start doing some math. I read, calculate numbers, and eat chocolate until all the candy is gone—sorry, neighborhood kids!—but I am left with an idea.

I pedal to school on Monday and of course one of the first people I see is Brooklyn. "Nice duds," she says when she passes me in the hall, and then exaggerates an explosive laugh as she and Hailey scurry off. I'm in my new blue daisy dress and green tights with an ivy pattern up the legs.

"Mrs. Otsawa!" I call, running to reach her. It may be my imagination, but it seems she's trying to outpace me. "Listen, I want to apologize for Friday," I say, grabbing her attention. "Also"—I point toward the quad—"that waste of water is an abomination."

She looks at me, eyebrows pitched, and then gazes toward the quad.

"I don't know why those sprinklers are on during the day," she says. "I'll need to speak to someone in utilities."

"Day, night, it doesn't matter," I say. "Do you know how many gallons it's taking to keep that grass alive?"

"Chloe," she says, "I'm very proud of our quad. It's the center of our school, and the students and the administration seem to really enjoy it. And once that oak tree grows, it will be even more beautiful. I don't think you—"

"But there are *new ways*," I say. "There are native plants, drought-resistant plants, real-looking Astroturf, which could all be just as beautiful and save gallons of water a day."

"I'm all for causes, and I appreciate you getting behind one. But not this one. How about helping me enforce the no-vaping rule?" she suggests. "Now that's one I can really get behind."

I don't answer her. I don't even know what to say. Instead, I race ahead to English and sit in the back row, drafting a letter during class, and at the next break I find my way to the computer lab, sit down, and look up GoFundMe online. Then I start a new project simply titled "Our Quad":

Though it is beautiful, our quad takes 40 gallons of water a week to keep it green, which adds up to more than 160 gallons a month, which is almost 2,000 gallons a year, and 20,000 gallons a decade. What if we replaced grass with Astroturf, succulents, and other drought-resistant native plants to create a sustainable garden?

Our administration is averse to change, and that's understandable. Each generation is resistant to change, and we will probably be resistant to change 40 years from now. But how about we take matters into our own hands and prove them wrong?

Every penny counts. Mother Nature thanks you for whatever you can afford. Won't you please contribute to saving our water and our planet and to improving our community?

Best,

A concerned student,

Chloe Tara Lovejoy

Chapter Fifteen

Panama City, Florida, and Pune, India, are pulsating weakly, so I create a small hurricane in Panama City before any more pressure mounts. I'm learning, and trying, and it's the best I can do for now. I program a light wind for our area, an ocean breeze. I circle the hologram, looking for the earth's needs. I step slowly and cautiously. Rain in Kauai. And lots of rainbows. Sunny and 70s in Dubai.

My GoFundMe is catching on. I already have $723 and some nice messages from classmates. Worthy cause, one says. Happy to contribute.

I join Mom in front of the television. She's watching *Jeopardy!*, but her eyes are glazed over and she's showing no expression.

“This gently sloping submerged portion of the continental margin extends from the shoreline to the continental slope,” the host says.

I know that! “What is the continental shelf?” I say.

None of the contestants answer it, but the host confirms that I am right.

“One of Earth’s compositional layers. The solid rocky shell that extends from the crust to the outer core.”

“What is the mantle?” I yell.

I am right again.

My mom looks toward me, but she doesn’t say anything.

The show cuts to a break for the news. “A small hurricane in Panama City today,” Duncan Sunshine says. “Sunny with a light coastal breeze here in Central Cali. News at ten!”

“He’s so handsome,” Mom says.

“Mother! Those teeth! They’re blinding they’re so white.” Leave it to Mom to crush on the cheeseball weatherman.

“Exactly,” Mom says. “I love a man who takes care of himself. Unlike your father.”

When *Jeopardy!* resumes, the host says, “This mountain-building event is related to plate collisions.”

“What is orogeny!” I answer.

“Now you’re just showing off,” Mom says, but I can tell she’s impressed.

In the school parking lot the next day, Brooklyn pulls over in her giant Mercedes. “What are you doing?” she asks, an edge in her voice, as usual.

“Locking my bike.”

"Since when did *you* become all 'save the planet'? That's *my* thing."

Well, at least I know she's seen my GoFundMe. I wonder if she contributed?

"What do you care?" I ask, fumbling with my lock, trying to get out of here as soon as possible.

"*I* was gonna propose a sustainable garden," she whines, "for my senior project, and now you went and pulled the rug right out from under me. I'm the one who donated the oak tree. I don't understand what's happening. Am I living in some alternative universe where *you* have progressive ideas? You've always just been so . . . so . . ."

"So *what*, Brooklyn?"

"So *basic*," she says too quickly.

She watches as I finish locking my bike and pocket the key. I don't want to start a screaming match or anything. I also don't want to end up in tears. I want to ignore her, but a storm is brewing inside; an internal volcano is two seconds away from erupting. And there are dark clouds overhead when there weren't any before.

"If you care so much about the environment, you should think of ditching your car and getting a bike," I suggest in a steady voice. It's taking everything in me to stay calm.

"Ditch my Mercedes?" she yells after me. "I don't think so!"

"Girls, girls!" It's my English teacher, Mr. Rosenberg. "What's going on here?"

"Who drives *that* in this day and age?" I snap. "It's not even a hybrid."

"And who drives *that*?" she snaps back, meaning my bike. "You're like a twelve-year-old!"

The sneer on her face is as vicious as any on a witch or evil stepmother I've seen in a movie or read about in a book. I'm starting to feel twitchy now. I'm letting her get to me, but I can't help it.

With Mr. Rosenberg watching us, a Shakespeare quote comes to mind, and I yell it at her. "You have such a February face," I say. "So full of frost, of storm and cloudiness."

She looks at me indignantly before peeling away in her big fat gas-guzzling tank.

Mr. Rosenberg laughs out loud. "Chloe!" he says as I feel raindrops on me. "A seventeenth-century insult in the twenty-first century. You have absolutely made my day—no, my year! I'm giving you extra credit whether you want it or not!"

I laugh with him. Of course I want extra credit. I need it.

"Brilliant," he says. "Just brilliant."

And I join the other kids heading inside, running because we all got caught in the rain.

It's Kortege's Chemistry midterm, but I haven't had a millisecond to study, as I've been studying something much bigger and more important—like, y'know, the earth. I cautiously open the exam, hoping I can get through it.

The answer to the first question is undoubtedly oxygen—the gas made up of two atoms that combines with other substances in "oxidation reactions" in order to release energy. How could I not know about oxygen when it combines with three atoms? Hello, ozone!

The next answer—hydrogen—is just a given. Number 1 on the periodic table.

The answer to the third question is fluorine, and I'm sure of this because it's what I consider to be the one of the most loathsome elements, due to its involvement with CFCs, chewing away at the precious ozone layer, the reason I ride a bike. But the question doesn't even cover that, only the fact that this element is part of a compound added to drinking water to help protect your teeth.

Next up: Mercury, number 80. Lithium, 3. Then sulfur, 16, which of course oozes from active volcanoes.

I love Chemistry! I think as I race through the test, identifying uranium, plutonium, and, of course, argon—the element assigned to me a few months ago, the one associated with an "inert atmosphere." Felix promised me I'd never forget this element, and, boy, was he right.

To my surprise, I'm the first one in the class to set my pencil down. I look around at the students who are still working. Some look confused. Others are erasing. Someone is even asleep.

I catch Mr. Kortege's eye, and I don't break the stare. I know what he's thinking—that I'm confused or failing or looking for an excuse to get out of the test, but I don't care. When he shifts his gaze down to his desk, I'm confident that my position in our complicated pecking order has changed, though I'm not sure exactly how.

When I exit class, I bump straight into Curtis. "Hey!" he says, looking me up and down. "I'm loving your vibe." Today, I'm wearing a dress with a cherry print and carrying my green grass purse. "Long time no see!"

"I know!" I say. *Don't fumble*, I tell myself. *You're Mother Freakin' Nature. Act it!*

"I contributed to your GoFundMe," he says. "Only twenty bucks, but, hey, it's something."

"Thank you so much!"

"So, question," he says. "You ever gonna come snowboarding with me up in Kismo?"

"I want to," I say. "I've just been really busy!"

"I know, I know. Junior year . . ."

"Yeah, that . . . and some other stuff."

"What's that saying? 'All work and no play . . .'"

"'Makes Jack a dull boy,'" Shannon says, passing us.

"Shan!" I call, but she keeps on walking. "Shan!" I yell louder.

"I'm sorry," I tell Curtis. "I'll be right back."

I weave through the hallway until I reach what used to be my best friend.

"Shannon!" I say. "Please don't ignore me." I motion for her to step into an empty classroom with me, and she hesitantly does.

"Looks like you're doing good forming sentences with Curtis," she says.

"I guess, but Shan—"

"Chlo—this is just a lot," she says, looking at the key around my neck.

"A lot," I echo. "It's so much."

"I don't know what to think."

"I get it."

"And now every time I hear something on the news, I'm wondering if it's your fault. That volcano in Washington? The hurricane in Panama City?"

"Can you come over later? Or sometime? You and Felix can come over and I'll try to show you what I'm dealing with. Maybe it'll make more sense . . ." I catch myself. "Or probably not, but still, I think you should come."

"Okay," she says. "How about tomorrow?"

"Yes!" I say. "Tomorrow."

"And Chlo? You went shopping without me?"

"I did," I say. "I'm sorry."

"I never would have let you buy that bag."

"It's cute!" I say.

"It's *grass*."

And we both start cracking up. How I've missed her! Her donkey laugh, the way she snorts and bounces her head up and down.

"Oh my God, I left Curtis back there. I gotta go," I say. "See you tomorrow."

Curtis is still standing there when I run back down the hall. But he's with Brooklyn, and I just can't deal, so I scurry in the opposite direction.

Chapter Sixteen

The little black box in the office is blinking. It's never done that before. I press the red button. "Hello?" I say tentatively. Wade's voice is on the other end.

"Chloe?" he says.

"I'm here."

"Hi," he says. "How's it going?"

I gaze around the space: the blinking lights in the hologram, *The Book of Nature* in the corner, the panels of rain activity, the cloud board, the rainbow swipes, the melting ice caps, the overwhelm of it all. "Fine?" I say in a small voice.

"I don't know how to say this, but you're going to need to

spend much, much more time in the Maparium. There are . . . hundreds . . . of imbalances, so you're going to have to closely monitor the situation over the next few days."

"I will," I say nervously.

"In HQ," he clarifies. "Not at school with the device. It needs your absolute full attention."

"Okay," I say. "When I get home from—"

"I don't think you're understanding me," he says. "Your *full* attention. School isn't your priority this week. Am I making myself clear?"

I've never heard Wade sound like this before, with an edge in his voice. "But I've got a bunch of—" I stop myself because I realize how unimportant any of it is to him. What does he care about my classes and quizzes and grades? Did he even go to school? I decide to keep my big mouth shut.

I stand over the hologram, trying to make sense of all the signals and signs. Something's quivering over China. I don't know how to defuse it.

I phone Shannon and leave a message. "I'm so sorry," I say. "Tomorrow's not gonna work for coming here. We'll do it another time, I promise." I press buttons, move levers, read more chapters in *The Book of Nature*.

An hour later, I'm burned-out, and I think I need a break.

Inside the house, I check my GoFundMe. It's swelled to over $2,000, with contributions from Mr. Kortege and even Mrs. Otsawa! Mom is in the kitchen, reading the newspaper, when I walk in to grab something to eat.

"What are you doing here?" I ask, knowing she's supposed to be at work.

Without making eye contact, she says, "I was let go."

Here it is again. I wonder what she's like in the workplace, where she's always getting "let go." Does she not listen to her boss? Does she talk back? Does she get drunk on the job?

"So sorry," I say, as I've said in the past.

"It just wasn't the right fit," she says, and I've heard that one before, too.

"You really didn't want to work for a bottled water company anyway," I say. "Those plastic bottles are showing up in oceans around the world and polluting sea life everywhere. Plastic is evil, seriously."

She narrows her eyes as she listens to me, and I can't tell if she wants to slap me or thank me.

"I'll find something else," she assures me. "I always do. And I do have some good news. I'm going on a date tonight."

How am I supposed to respond to that?

"Hello?" she says. "Did you hear me?"

"You're going on a date. I heard."

"Don't you want to know with who?"

"With *whom*," I correct.

"Someone famous. A weatherman."

"What? Not Duncan Sunshine, I hope."

I'm joking. At least I thought I was until she starts nodding yes.

"You're going on a date with Duncan Sunshine, the cheesiest weatherman, who always gets the weather wrong?"

"You mean the handsome man with the perfect teeth," she says. "The bottled water company sponsored his show last week, and we went to his news set, and he and I got to talking, and he asked me out."

"Before you got fired," I add. Then I quickly realize I've hurt her feelings. "Sorry," I say, trying to practice empathy.

"Teenage girls," she says, shaking her head. "Try to cut you to the quick every single time. I'm going upstairs to get ready. He's picking me up at seven, and I suggest you stay far away if you don't have anything nice to say."

"It's four thirty," I say. I guess it takes her that long to pull herself together. "Don't worry," I promise. "I will."

Over the next week, I wake up every morning at six and after breakfast make my way to the Maparium. I start the day tending to the boards. The floods in Tennessee, the heat wave in London. I'm trying to find balance. Sometimes, I forget to shower, to eat, to move. I'm sure school is calling, Mrs. Otsawa dialing our number on repeat. But Mom's barely home, instead going on multiple day dates with Duncan. Gag. I wake up, eat, go to the Maparium, watch for signals and signs, go to bed, wake up, and do it all over again. I've lost track of time, but I don't even care. Maybe school is one of the sacrifices I'll need to make, my dreams of college slowly fading into the background.

Is it day or night when an alarm pierces the air, intrusive and deafening? I've never heard this sound before, and my heart starts galloping. It's so loud and persistent. Is it another earthquake? I'm sure the neighbors can hear.

I press the intercom, hoping to contact Wade. "Hello? Hello?" I say, but there's no reply. Or maybe there is but the alarm is so loud it's drowning it out.

I take the elevator up, assuming I'll find Mom trying to break in again, but instead I see two shadows and hear the muffled voices of Felix and Shannon outside. When I open the door a crack, the alarm stops.

"Oh my God," Felix says. "That noise!"

"You guys!" I say.

"You're so pale," Shannon says, looking concerned.

"I'm fine," I say too quickly. "Especially now that I can hear again."

"We were worried," Felix says. "Can we come in? What's that smell?"

It's probably me. I haven't showered in days. The place is a mess, but I guess it's time for me to reveal my truth. I open the door wide and usher them in.

"Whoa," Shannon says, her eyes bulging.

I look around and try to imagine what she's thinking. I still have to remind myself that this is all real. "This is the office," I tell her. "The Maparium is downstairs."

"An elevator!" Felix says. "Here?"

All three of us step in.

When the elevator has descended and the doors open, the spinning hologram is the first thing in sight. Through my friends' eyes, I see how magical it is all over again. I whisper as I show them around. I don't want Wade knowing I've let outsiders in. I lead them to the rainbow board and swipe an arc over Dublin.

"I'm still learning," I explain.

"Listen," Felix says. "You need vitamin D. C'mon, you've been down here too long. Let's get you out in real nature."

"I can't," I say. "I have so much to do. I have to watch over everything."

"Don't you have that portable thing?" he asks. He motions for me to grab it.

Since Wade hasn't been answering on the intercom, I figure I can maybe sneak out for an hour. I pocket the device, and we ride up the elevator. I lock the office with my key, relieved to hear the distinct *click*.

Being with my friends is like breathing clean air. They take me to the park where we all used to play when we were younger, the same one Grandma and I used to go to. A pair of birds appears above only me as we swing on the swings facing Morro Rock. I notice but don't call attention to it.

We drive to the beach. "Can you make the waves bigger?" Felix suggests.

"I don't know how to do that," I say.

"Look it up or something!" he says.

I scroll through my device until I get to *W*. There are electronic levers to move, but also there is a chant. "Fluctus maior," I say. The waves start getting bigger. A surfer runs in, and then a few minutes later a bunch more.

The three of us watch, speechless.

We walk the path on the marina boardwalk, and I point out the egrets, sandpipers, and willets.

"Remember when you were scared of birds?" Shannon asks.

"Anything with wings, really," Felix says.

"Not anymore," I tell them. "They're miraculous."

It feels good to be interacting with real nature instead of technology. There are so many places on the map that I want to travel to: Costa Rica, Hawaii, Niagara Falls. I don't come from a traveling kind of family, like Shannon and Felix do, but now I want to see the whole world.

As the sun starts to set, we head home, passing our school on the way. It's a Saturday and no one's on campus. Felix hops the fence to the quad and lets us in through the gate.

We approach the young oak tree Brooklyn paid for last year when she was just starting her "make sure I get into a good college" environmental kick.

"Wanna see something cool?" I say, hoping it might work.

Both my friends nod.

I remember Grandma making lemons sprout from the tree in our backyard, yellow globes suddenly bursting from the branches after her chant.

"Crescere arbor," I try.

Nothing happens.

I say it again.

Still nothing.

"Whatever you're saying, say it with power," Felix suggests. "You sound too meek!"

"Crescere arbor?" I say again, and I think I see the tree quiver.

"Oh my God," Shannon says. "What was that? Say it again, but not like a question!"

"Crescere arbor," I say, this time lifting my hands like a conductor, the way Grandma did.

The oak tree starts growing and expanding, its branches reaching up and out like arms, its trunk gaining height.

The three of us shriek in joy—and a bit of terror.

"Look what you did!" Felix says.

"How?" Shannon screams.

When I say it one more time—"Crescere arbor!"—I yell it so loud I bet people on Mount Kismo must have heard, and I hear my voice echo throughout the neighborhood.

"Chloe!" Shannon laughs. "Chloe!"

And now the tree has sprouted ten feet higher, majestic and mighty, right there in the middle of the quad, a canopy of leaves and a thick, sturdy trunk.

"Mother Freakin' Nature!" Shannon yells. "It really is you!"

Chapter Seventeen

Things feel more under control in the office, so I go to school on Monday. Everyone's surrounding the oak tree in awe, and Brooklyn is in the center of it all. "I paid for this magical tree," she tells the crowd. "I knew it was special. Takes one to know one."

"I've never seen anything like this," Mrs. Otsawa says, gazing up at the leaves and branches. "Unless we were all too busy to notice it was growing incrementally. This doesn't make any sense!"

Mr. Kortege takes samples from the bark. Shannon, Felix, and I watch from the sidelines, pleased that our experiment has yielded results.

"This is amaze-balls," Shannon sings.

"This is my tree," Brooklyn tells anyone who will listen. Then she wraps her arms around the trunk, and everyone takes her picture.

After lunch, Curtis approaches me. "Did you ever read that book *A Tree Grows in Brooklyn*?"

I shake my head no. "But I've heard of it."

"A sequel can be *Brooklyn Grows a Tree*."

"Ha ha," I say, though I'm just humoring him.

"It's pretty surreal," he says. "A tree that she bought suddenly sprouts on campus overnight? What's happening with your sustainable garden project?" he asks. "Did you raise enough money?"

"I haven't checked in a few days," I say. "Do you have a cell?"

"Of course," he says. "Wait, do you not?"

"Not with me."

"That's so cool," he says. "I'm addicted to mine."

What he doesn't know is that I can't keep track of the phone *and* the device, so I've left my phone at home.

He reaches for his, and we navigate to my GoFundMe page and see the latest total.

"Chloe!" he says. "You're at $9,210.33! You just need another eight hundred dollars."

"In twenty-four hours," I say, disappointed.

"C'mon, we can do it. What if eight teachers donated one hundred dollars?"

"I think that's more than they make," I say.

"What if we get someone to sponsor this, like, like . . . the news, or Duncan Sunshine!"

"Oh my gosh," I say. "That's a great idea, and I actually have a connection to him, believe it or not." I lean in closer and whisper, "My mom is dating him."

"No way!" he says, laughing. "Do they talk about the weather?"

"I'm sure it comes up."

"Why don't you give it a try? Okay, so I'm officially asking again . . . do you ever want to come up to Kismo and go boarding?"

"It sounds like so much fun. But (a) I don't snowboard, and (b) I'm a little scared of heights."

"Not a problem! I've been told I'm an excellent teacher."

"Well, but (c) I . . . um . . . have . . ."

Lots of work to do. Ugh. It sounds so basic, so boring. Like the stupidest of excuses. I want to go. I really do.

"Can I let you know later this week?" I say.

"Right on," he says, smiling wide.

That night, as I'm eating dinner alone in the kitchen, Mom breezes past me wearing a sexy off-the-shoulder black dress. "Have a good night. I'm going out to dinner with Dunc."

"Again?"

"Yes, again. This time he's taking me to La Rouix. Don't wait up," she sings.

Shouldn't I be the one having fun? Why is she going out every single night while I'm drowning in schoolwork and stuck behind the boards in the Maparium?

Balance and harmony, I hear a voice in my head say. But I don't have either, and I need at least one.

"Can I ask you something, Mom?"

"Go ahead," she says, blotting some lipstick.

"I'm raising money for a sustainable garden on campus, and we're looking for a sponsor for the last eight hundred dollars."

Mom looks surprised. "That's very proactive," she says, almost like it's a bad thing.

"Maybe on your date tonight you could ask . . ."

"You want me to ask Duncan?" she says.

I nod.

"I would never," she says, offended. "We just started dating. I can't ask him for money."

But the next morning when I check the account, there's an $800 contribution from Anonymous, who wrote: Environmental warriors are my favorite warriors.

I run into Mrs. Otsawa's office and ask to use her computer, where I open my account and show her I've sourced the funds. "We have enough for a sustainable garden," I say excitedly. "Ten thousand dollars!"

"Chloe Lovejoy," she says, sounding impressed. "You really put your money where your mouth is. I am pleased to see you so engaged this semester."

"So we can do it? We can hire someone to replace the grass and stuff?"

"I have another idea," she says. "I think we should have our entire community participate. Make the whole community feel part of the project."

Over the next couple of weeks, there are wheelbarrows in the quad at all hours, and my teachers and classmates take turns digging up the grass and replacing it with fake stuff, and planting wildflowers like California poppies, milkweed, Pacific wax myrtle, and shrubby monkey flower. The yellows, crimsons and pinks, oranges, and greens combine to bring our quad to life.

Our school paper, *The Breeze,* does a photo essay about it, and the local TV station picks up the story, sending a van to school during lunch on a Thursday. Out walks a cameraman, followed by Duncan Sunshine, in the flesh! He's shorter than he looks on TV. His teeth are gleaming in the bright sun. His face is too tan, and his hair looks fake. I wonder if I should introduce myself, or if he already knows to seek me out.

I watch as he approaches Mrs. Otsawa. She keeps smiling extra-wide and touching him on the shoulder, and then they both gaze across the quad until they lock eyes with me. At least I think they're looking at me. I glance over my shoulder, just in case it's someone else, and when I turn back, they are definitely coming my way.

"There she is," Mrs. Otsawa says. "This is Chloe Lovejoy, instigator of this entire endeavor." After her introduction, she darts off to talk to someone calling to her from the other side of the quad.

Duncan reaches his hand out for me to shake it. "Well, if it isn't the infamous Chloe," he says.

Infamous: adjective, well-known for a bad quality or deed.

"Infamous?" I say. "Or famous?"

He laughs like he does on TV. "You're beautiful Laurel Lovejoy's daughter," he says. "It is my great honor to meet you."

I shake his limp hand.

"Can I get you on camera saying a few things about this spectacular garden?"

"I guess," I say. I'm holding the device, so I reach over for my bag to place it in.

"Is that your cell phone?" he asks too quickly.

"No, no, it's . . . a . . . hard drive."

I watch him watch me rest it carefully in my grass bag. Maybe I'm being paranoid, but I don't put my bag on the ground. Instead, I keep it over my shoulder.

The cameraman appears, and Duncan leans toward me. "We're going live. Just follow along," he says, and then turns to the camera. "April showers bring May flowers, but not in this case! This time, October drought brings November flowers, thanks to Chloe Lovejoy, a high school junior and a nature warrior." He shoves a mic in my face. "Tell us about this, Chloe."

"Oh, um . . . well, water was the main reason I started this, because I realized it takes forty gallons—"

"Yes," he says. "Water. Wasting water. Bad. Very bad."

"I started a GoFundMe, and chose plants and flowers that required little to no water to—"

"Yoo-hoo! Mr. Sunshine!" we suddenly hear.

We both turn around and see Brooklyn in the oak tree. She's actually climbed a few branches and is sitting there on a limb with her friend Hailey.

"Mr. Sunshine, come interview me in my magical oak tree. You won't believe this story!"

Duncan looks into the camera. "Seems we have two nature warriors!" he says, laughing. "Nothing like live television. Let's go see what's in the tree over here . . ."

And just like that, they move over to Brooklyn. In the tree that grew big and tall thanks to *me*. Surrounded by the garden that was *my* idea. That girl is constantly ruining my life.

"I'm going to be holding a climate rally on the winter solstice," she says into the camera, as though she's practiced all her life for this moment. "We'll start at the Embarcadero and march to Morro Rock, and I hope your viewers will join us in bringing awareness to climate change heading into the new year."

"What a great idea," Duncan says as the cameraman zooms in on her face.

"Thank you." She smiles, one eye on the camera, one eye on me.

Chapter Eighteen

My favorite part of being Mother Nature is playing with clouds on the cloud board. I could spend hours there, designing big, billowy ones or trailing little wisps. Sometimes, I cover the sun in Honduras with clouds, and other times I slide them all out of the way, making space for a perfect day. When I was younger, I would lie down on a towel in the backyard and marvel at the billowy clouds above—seeing Mickey Mouse, a princess, a bear—never ever entertaining the thought that Grandma was in the office orchestrating everything for my pleasure.

I'm spending a lot of time in the Maparium again, because school's out for the Thanksgiving break. It's our first Thanksgiving without Grandma. Mom tried to get me to spend it with her and Duncan Sunshine, but I put an end to it as soon as she said, "What do you think about—"

"That would be a definite no," I said, lifting my hand for her to stop.

Instead, Dad decided he'd come over and we could all spend it together as a fake family, over the turkey I'll inevitably be too stressed out to eat.

Dad makes smashed brussels sprouts, and they're actually delicious—I didn't know he had it in him—and Mom sets out a nice table. I try extra hard to be thankful for everything and everyone. I try so hard.

And when I can't try anymore, I retreat to the office to dust the East Coast with snow, leaving my parents in the kitchen talking about God knows what.

"How are you doing today?" Wade asks the next day. While everyone's shopping Black Friday sales, I'm still in the office working.

"I don't know," I confess. "How am I supposed to be doing?"

"I can't answer that," he says. "I realized it's your first Thanksgiving without your grandma, and it must be hard."

"It is, actually."

"It's been wonderful for the earth, having your full attention these past couple of days," he says.

I know what he means. I understand. When I'm here, focused and present, the earth *does* seem to respond. There have been fewer disasters, as far as I can tell, and things seem to be working in sync. It's not something I can explain; it's a feeling. There is balance, and there is harmony—and not only with the earth, but also within me.

I do miss Grandma tonight as I sit here alone in the Maparium, so many lights twinkling and pulsating, the earth oblivious to the fact that it's a holiday, simply calling out like a hungry baby. Still, the hologram is calm tonight, and so am I.

I decide to program some snow in my neighborhood. Just a dusting—nothing too dramatic, not a blizzard or anything.

I run outside to watch the fat flakes spill to the ground. The perfection in which they fall reminds me of the upside of my job. I see kids and parents running out of their homes, too, laughing in delight, and I feel like a good citizen, like Santa Claus. I step back into the house to see what Duncan Sunshine has to say about this.

I snap on the TV in Grandma's room.

"Folks! It's a winter wonderland here in Morro Bay," Duncan says. "Such a rare event in our part of the world." Then his expression changes. As he looks into the camera, it feels like he's looking directly at me. "Wonderland. Wonder why? Mother Nature sure has some tricks up her sleeve!"

I click him off.

Chapter Nineteen

As soon as Thanksgiving is over, our town explodes in Christmas lights. Lights on houses, on shops, in parks, and on the boats bobbing in the harbor. Morro Bay starts twinkling as soon as the sun goes down, which is before five o'clock these days. Sparkling lights everywhere.

"So, your mom's dating Duncan Sunshine?" Brooklyn says as we approach Life Skills.

How would she know that?

"My mom saw them in the grocery store, making out by the fresh herbs."

“Whatever,” I say, trying to blow her off.

“Will you be the bridesmaid if they get married?” Brooklyn asks. “I mean you already have a bunch of flowery dresses.”

My breathing quickens. I muscle past her into class and take a seat in the circle as far away from her as possible. In my state of nervous energy, I reach for the Talking Stick.

“Uh-uh,” Ms. Hampton says. “Not yet, Chloe. You don’t even know what today’s subject is.”

As the rest of my classmates join the circle, I run a few scenarios in my mind. My mom and Duncan in the produce department, unable to contain themselves, Duncan bending over to kiss her, parsley and thyme in the background.

“Good afternoon, class,” Ms. Hampton says. “Namaste to all.”

Why does Mom go for the worst guys? And why does the detail about the fresh herbs make me so angry?

“Today we’re going to talk about goals. I want you to think about your five-year plan, and what goals you’ll need to reach it. Chloe, you seemed eager to grab the Talking Stick, so why don’t you go first?”

The weatherman can’t know I’m Mother Nature, especially when he thinks he owns the weather. Mom wouldn’t have had the nerve to tell him about my gig, would she?

“Chloe?” she says. “Talking Stick?”

“Um, that’s okay,” I say. “I’d rather not go first.”

“Oh, but I thought—”

“I will,” Brooklyn says, reaching for it.

And as I picture Duncan Sunshine in my house, my life, in my business, I hear Brooklyn in the background, like white noise, detailing her four years at Harvard, followed by her starting an environmental nonprofit, thinking she's going to change the world.

At home, I dump my books and go to the kitchen to grab something to eat. My head is deep in the fridge when Mom walks in, whistling. I find some string cheese and slam the door shut.

"Oh, you're home!" she says.

I blurt out, "What's this about you and Duncan Sunshine making out at the supermarket?"

Mom tilts her head and smiles, a faraway look in her eyes. "How did you hear that?" She laughs like a teenager.

"Someone at school told me."

"He likes for us to be seen together out in public," she says.

Out together in public by the fresh herbs, according to Brooklyn.

"You'd think he'd be more private, since he's a celebrity. But nope! His house is exquisite," she tells me. "You should see it."

"I'm not moving anywhere, if that's what you're getting at," I say, and point to the backyard. "Helloooo."

"Moving anywhere?" she says. "Look who's jumping to conclusions. Sheesh!"

"Whatever," I say.

"He's taking me somewhere special this weekend. A surprise getaway."

"Have fun," I say.

"Don't you worry. I will."

We are rehearsing the Journey song in Chorus today, and I have to admit we are sounding extra-fab. The harmonies are pitch-perfect.

The altos start the first three lines of the song, and the sopranos sing the next three, and then we build slowly and steadily until we reach the chorus. I can sense the anticipation as we get ready to belt out the chorus. Hearing all of our voices together gives me chills.

It also gives me a boost of confidence, and as we exit class I approach Curtis.

"Hi," I say. "Remember your snowboarding offer?"

"Of course."

"Is it still a possibility?"

"So, you're ready for a lesson?" he asks.

"I'm in. What are you doing on Saturday?"

"I'm going up to Kismo Friday. I'm so psyched you can come!"

On the way out the door, I hum the part of the song about everybody wanting a thrill.

I hunt down Felix. "Okay," I say when I find him by his locker. "So I've been invited to go snowboarding with Curtis Reed. Do you want to come?"

"What? And be your third wheel? No, thanks," he says, slamming his locker closed.

"Not a third wheel," I say, but I know I sound unconvincing.

"Trust me, you don't want me there. And, trust me, I don't want to be there. I don't snowboard."

"Me neither."

"I don't ski," he says. "I don't really do snow."

"And you want to go to college in New York?"

"That's *slush*," he explains. "City slush is the exception to my rule."

Okay, time to change my approach.

"I need a ride," I say. "That's the God's honest truth. I mean, I can't get there on my bike, and Curtis is going on Friday."

Felix takes a hard look at me. "Oh, okay, now I get it." He has relaxed his tone. "Sure," he says. "You went with me to the Harvest Dance. I owe you."

It's that easy? "Thank you so much," I say, reaching up to hug him. It feels so good settling on the truth.

Chapter Twenty

On Saturday morning, I sync the device, and make sure the battery is full. In the Maparium, I address what I have time for, but today I am determined to be an average sixteen-year-old tearing down the mountain—if only for a few hours. If nature is about finding balance and harmony, and I am part of nature, then I need to find my own balance and harmony, because lately it seems as if I've only been about imbalance and discord. I am determined to have a carefree day on the mountain with Curtis.

"I'll be back later," I call before walking out the front door. I'm not even sure if Mom's still home, though her car is in the driveway.

Each mile Felix and I drive takes me farther from the Maparium: the spinning globes, the illuminated maps, the banks of levers, and the one solitary small black intercom that links me with my mentor. *It's gonna be fine,* I assure myself, but my breathing is getting heavier. Grandma must have vacated the Maparium at some point in her life to have a little fun; I can't be the first.

"Why's it steaming in here?" Felix says, rolling down his window.

"I'm a little warm," I say, fanning myself. I'm actually sweating with nerves.

We drive past school, the giant oak tree visible over the gate, then past the railroad station, the farmers' market, and the lumberyard downtown. Then we merge onto the highway, which will eventually lead us up the mountain.

I stare at the black oaks and sugar maples, naked without their leaves but still standing proud, and then gaze at the pine trees—ponderosa, Jeffrey—and their pine-cone nuggets, some tucked throughout the branches but most, having fallen, now resting at the base of the trees. All the fir trees, their fragrant needles waving in the wind. It's a picture postcard, this landscape, a perfect snow globe. This mountain is so much a part of my grandmother, her ashes now resting peacefully on the forest bed, and so much a part of me.

"Do you think I should have gotten chains for my tires?" Felix asks.

"Nah," I say. I made sure to keep the snow at the *top* of the mountain.

I am so relieved to be out of my house, away from the Maparium. My cares begin to evaporate with every mile.

When Curtis opens the front door to his cute A-frame cabin, he looks genuinely happy to see us. He and Felix fist-bump hello. "Glad you could make it!" Curtis says, taking our bags and leading us inside.

The cabin has that musty smell that somehow screams cozy. It confirms that I am on vacation. There is a family photo of the Reeds, framed and hanging over the fireplace—Mom, Dad, Curtis, and a sister. I step in to take a closer look, examining their features and all of their curls.

I head to the bathroom. In the mirror, I tuck my hair behind my ears and take a good look at myself. Something has changed, but I can't identify what it is. My hair is longer, that much is obvious, but there's something subtler in my face. I lean in close and inspect my forehead, my eyebrows, my eyes, then my nose, cheeks, and lips, and yet nothing alone looks that different. Overall, though, the sum of my parts has transformed somehow.

I tilt my head and smile. I am here, in Curtis Reed's bathroom, in his mountain house, about to spend a day on the slopes with him. I can finally talk to him without feeling flustered.

Before I forget, I adjust the device to allow a steady dusting of fresh powder for my lesson, and I stride to the living room, ready to start this glorious day.

Then Brooklyn Weber is standing there with her friend Hailey.

I feel my face melt into a frown.

"Well, looky what the cat dragged in," Brooklyn says when she notices me, her blond hair cascading down her back, an adorable pink beanie atop her head.

Felix and Curtis are also in the living room. Felix's eyebrows are raised as if he's watching the best show on television. How long was I in the bathroom that this could have transpired?

"We were in the neighborhood and thought we'd stop by," Brooklyn says. "I had no idea *you'd* be here."

"No idea," Hailey echoes, eyeing me.

I join Felix and Curtis on the couch, trying to play it cool.

"How did you know my address?" Curtis asks nervously.

"I remember you said your folks had a place in Kismo," Brooklyn says. "So do Hailey's parents. They did some sleuthing. There's only one Reed family up here."

Hailey seems embarrassed. "Only after you asked them t—"

Brooklyn whacks her friend in the arm.

"What size shoe are you?" Curtis asks me.

"Seven and a half," Brooklyn says.

"Not you," Curtis says.

"Six," I say.

"Perfect," he says. "So is my sister. You can borrow her boots and her snowboard, so you won't have to rent anything."

"Oh, you're a newbie?" Brooklyn asks me. "They have good teachers up here. Curtis, we should go to Devil's Peak while they're on the bunny hill."

"Curtis is my teacher," I clarify.

"And mine," Felix adds.

Hailey says, "I'm more of a sip-hot-chocolate-and-watch-all-the-cuties-in-the-lodge type of girlie."

"Sounds riveting," I say.

We rent gear for Felix at the lodge and drop Hailey off by the fireplace. I'm inwardly raging as the four of us ride up the chairlift. I hate heights, so I cling to the bar and stare straight ahead. *If the chair falls, I'll land in snow,* I tell myself, grasping tighter. Not that I want any of that to happen.

"Perfect conditions," Brooklyn says, tying her thick hair into a topknot and replacing her beanie, totally carefree in our dangling chair.

I start feeling even more nervous as we're preparing to get off the lift. I tried skiing once when I was little, but this will be my first time snowboarding. The last thing I need is to fall flat on my face in front of Curtis. But much to my surprise he takes my hand, or rather my glove, as the chair reaches the exit point, and drags my teetering self to safety.

Instead, it's Felix who takes a tumble.

"Man down!" the lift operator screams, and stops the chairs so they don't hit him. Still, Felix nearly gets whacked in the head with Brooklyn's snowboard as she trips over him to safety.

"You okay, man?" Curtis says, taking his elbow and hoisting him up. Felix's body and face are caked in snow.

"No," he says, glaring at me.

Brooklyn is down the hill before we even get the rest of our gear on.

A few minutes later, as Curtis is patiently teaching us how to balance on a snowboard, she calls to us from the lift. "I'm going to Devil's Peak, losers!"

"Right where you belong," Felix says under his breath.

It's not like I've got the hang of it or anything, but I'm starting to feel a little bit confident, like I can at least see the *potential* for fun. Curtis keeps telling me to relax into it, not to stiffen up, and I have to keep reminding myself that I'm not on skis, that both legs need to work in unison if I want to make it down the mountain without tipping over. When I gain momentum, I make wide turns as the board scrapes down the hill.

I love it up here. I love being normal me on a regular Saturday, no responsibilities but to learn how to snowboard.

"You're doing so awesome," Curtis says, whooshing past me.

A few minutes later, Brooklyn skids to a stop at the bottom of the hill, snow splattering our faces. "It's beyond," she tells Curtis. "You gotta come up for just one run."

"I can't yet," he says.

"Just one," she says, taking him by the arm. "Then you can come back to the bunny hill to continue with your little pet project." She laughs. "Bunny hill, pet project . . ."

"It's okay," he says, wriggling out of her grasp.

I try to take a step back, but for a second I forget that I'm tethered to my board, and I lose my balance, tipping over sideways—*splat*—into the snow.

Curtis and Brooklyn are both gazing down at me. Brooklyn forces a laugh. "What are you, drunk?"

She did not just say that. She did not just trigger every issue I've ever had with my mother. "I have to go to the bathroom," I say, trying to stand. I don't want Curtis to see that I'm about to cry.

He holds out his hand to help me up. I brush the snow from my pants. Without saying anything else, I detach from my board and trudge into the lodge.

"I'll meet you in there!" Curtis calls, and I hear his footsteps behind me. But I don't turn around. Instead, I walk quicker and quicker ahead, passing Hailey sipping on cocoa in front of the fireplace.

I step into the restroom and into a stall. I don't know if it's because I'm layered in a million winter clothes, but I'm starting to sweat again. I'm so hot I feel like I'm going to faint. In nature, there are always predators and prey, and I'm tired of Brooklyn's predatory nature and I am so tired of being her prey.

I close my eyes, and I have a vision of Brooklyn at the top of Devil's Peak. She's beginning to board down, and I visualize what a pile of snow would look like rumbling behind her, chasing her, catching her, knocking her to the ground.

I know I shouldn't, but I surreptitiously take the device out of my pocket and glance at it. *Just looking,* I tell myself.

I identify Devil's Peak on the map in a few seconds. Quickly, I create a little squall, to knock Brooklyn off her game. I add a small earthquake to the mix, and program it in an hour from now. Just a wee one, as Grandma used to say whenever there was a little rumbler.

When I'm done, I pocket the device, wash my hands, and exit the bathroom. I push my way outside, past the crowds in the restaurant, and spot Felix.

"There you are," we both say in unison.

"I've been looking all over for you," Felix says.

"And me you. Where's Curtis?"

"He said he was going to do a quick run."

"What? He was just behind me."

"That was, like, half an hour ago, Chloe. You were gone forever!" he says. "Everything okay?"

"Yes," I assure him, but he knows me better than that.

"Curtis went up to Devil's Peak."

"No, he didn't."

"Okay," Felix says. "But he did."

I grab him by the hand and drag him onto the chairlift.

"I can't believe you," he says. "Why are you doing this to me?"

Because nature will take its course and we'll be out of harm's way, I think. *And we have to get Curtis before he heads down.*

"It's just a mountain and snow," I say instead. "If I can do it, so can you."

The chair creaks its way up the mountain. We have another forty-five minutes until my squall and wee earthquake start. We'll stall near the chairlift since I programmed it deeper in the woods. It's so quiet and pretty up here. I'm reveling in the peace.

"What's that?" Felix says, pointing. "Down there. It looks like they're filming something."

And when I follow his finger, I see a bunch of people surrounding a man and a woman, and the man is bending down on one knee, and the woman is . . .

The woman is my mother.

Chapter Twenty-One

"Mom!" I yell from the chair. I'm clutching the bar because I'm so dizzy.

"Chloe, she can't hear you," Felix says.

"*Mother!*" I roar. "Noooo!"

And then, from very far away, I hear a rumble, like a large truck is passing by, and then a horn blasting through the entire area of the mountain. What is that? A really horrible feeling washes over me. Is it my squall? But it's too early. It's not supposed to happen for another forty minutes. I grab the device from my pocket and glance at the data, but there's so much blinking I can't process it all.

It happens so fast, the rumble noise, which gives way to a cloud of snow in the distance, like a massive frozen waterfall cascading over a steep cliff. And it's heading straight toward the Devil's Peak chairlift.

"Oh my God!" Felix yells.

The posts holding up the lift cave like matchsticks. I'm seeing it all, but it happens so fast I still don't understand.

And then we hear one of the lift operators yell at the top of his lungs, "Avalanche!"

Felix and I exchange terrified glances as our chair comes to a complete stop and we are left dangling in midair.

"What did you do?" he demands.

I programmed a squall. A small storm. Like, the tumbleweed of storms. Not an avalanche. I never wrote avalanche into the device. I know the difference.

"Chloe! Tell me. Honestly," Felix says. "What did you do?"

"Not this," I say.

It seems everyone who was once on the mountain is now at the bottom of it, and now we are, too. Everyone's crowding us—skiers, snowboarders, parents, kids. We can make out snippets of conversation: "happened so fast," and "Devil's Peak," and "force of the snow," and "definitely people down."

Felix manages to disentangle from his snowboard. "God, I hate mountain sports," he says, throwing it to the ground. "We better get out of here."

"People down? How did this happen? What about Curtis?" I say.

"He'll find us inside."

We make our way back into the ski lodge with hordes of other people, where televisions are blaring breaking news. "An avalanche has struck on Mount Kismo," someone on TV says. "Just so rare in this part of the world."

I didn't mean for *this* to happen. Something, but not this epic fail. Hailey runs toward us. "Where's Brooklyn?" she cries.

I gaze around, searching for Curtis. Where are my mother and Duncan Sunshine? Everyone in the lodge looks shell-shocked as they tilt their heads toward the TV screens.

Suddenly, I see a pink ski cap. Brooklyn approaches, robot-like, her face blotchy.

"Thank God," Hailey says, falling into her arms.

"Curtis is missing," Brooklyn says breathlessly when she finds me. "I was about to go down Devil's Peak when he called out to me from the lift. He told me to wait for him."

"He couldn't have been on the lift," I say. Felix said he was probably on his way down the hill as we were riding up. I'm panting like an animal—a dog, a cheetah, a bobcat.

"He'll be fine," Felix says to Brooklyn. "Don't be a drama queen."

But I can tell from the blank expression on her face that she's dead serious.

"I thought I just saw him," I say, looking around frantically. I'm searching for curly hair and rosy cheeks, and seeing them everywhere. But none of them belong to Curtis. And where is my mother? Why don't I see her anywhere?

"You're not hearing me," she says, louder. "I saw him. I saw him on the ski lift, and then there was no ski lift."

Felix sits Brooklyn down at a crowded table.

He's not dead, I keep telling myself as I glance between the TV screens and Brooklyn. She's now shivering, and Felix is reluctantly running his hands up and down her arms to warm her up.

I run outside. Felix calls after me, but I don't stop. Soon, a snowmobile zooms down the hill, carrying a covered body, and police do their best to clear everyone out of the way.

Please, no, I beg. *Please don't let this be Curtis.*

But it dawns on me that even if it's not Curtis, it's *someone*. And by the looks of it, a dead someone.

A dead someone. Dead because of me? The sight of this causes me to collapse to the ground.

I think back to the life cycle of a frog chart Mrs. Brewer drew on the chalkboard when I was in second grade: the egg, which became a tadpole and then sprang into a froglet, which then grew into a frog, and then death. I'd raised my hand and asked what I thought was an obvious question, since I was staring at a circle. "What happens between death and when it becomes the egg again?" But Mrs. Brewer said curtly, "Nothing happens. That's what death means."

"Chloe!" Felix shouts.

Death. Mother Nature causes death. I know, but now I *know*.

"Chlo-eee," he says.

I hear him. I hear his voice getting closer, and I hear commotion around me, but I can't stand up and I can't speak. I just lie silently in the snow, not even feeling the cold.

I wake in a hospital bed, and Brooklyn is seated on a chair next to me. When will this nightmare be over?

"You fainted," she tells me, annoyed. "You're dehydrated."

"Mom?" I say. And I'm so scared to hear her response. I'm trying to read Brooklyn's face, but it's stony and unrevealing, as usual. I look around the room. "Where's my hard drive?" I say, sitting up.

"I'm definitely not your mom," she says. "And you're obsessed with this thing. You kept asking about it in the ambulance. It's with your clothes on that chair," she says, pointing. "Felix went back to Curtis's cabin and got everything for you."

Only then do I realize I'm in a blue hospital gown, an IV attached to my arm.

"Curtis is on the fourth floor," she says. "He has a broken clavicle and a torn shoulder and ACL. He has to have surgery."

"And my mom?" I ask weakly.

"She's on this floor," she says. "She has a concussion. The weatherman's here, too!"

"They're alive?" I say. A rush of adrenaline courses through me. I feel tears well up from the bottom of my feet.

"So far," Brooklyn says.

I gaze toward the little black device.

"Why are you here?" I ask.

"Hailey went to get her car," she says. "Thirty-seven people were injured, and someone died. This is the first time there's ever been an avalanche up here. I can't believe I was two minutes away from being caught in it. And the fact that Curtis survived is a miracle."

Thirty-seven people injured and one dead? Because of me? Happy-go-lucky skiers just enjoying their day. And then . . . and then . . .

The television is on in the background. I see images from the slopes. Snowmobiles zooming up the mountain, police in the lodge, dangling chairlifts, piles of snow. There are videos from people's cell phones. The sheer force of the avalanche caught on camera, people crying and in shock.

Brooklyn starts whimpering. "I don't understand."

I start crying, too, overwhelmed by this stupid day, by this reality. I can't do this. I shouldn't do this. I wipe away my tears. My one day of freedom dissolved into this. A life ended. All my fault. I've never even killed a fly.

More images are streaming onto the TV. They are interviewing the wife and child of someone who's missing. They are not crying, but they look frozen in shock. The little girl is looking up at her mom. I can't bear it.

Felix walks into the room with a half-eaten Snickers bar as I rip the IV out of my arm.

"Chloe!" he says, alarmed.

"You can't do that!" Brooklyn says.

"I have to find my mom," I say. "I'm sure I'm hydrated enough now."

I run to the chair and zip back up into my wet clothes. All I have for shoes are the snowboarding boots that Curtis loaned me, so I put them on and hobble around the small room. I shove the device deep into my pocket.

"C'mon," I say.

Felix follows me, leaving Brooklyn in there alone, watching the news. We amble down the hallway, and that's when I see him: Duncan Sunshine. He's on his cell phone outside my mom's room. When he sees me, he hangs up. "You're Chloe, right?" he says. "Laurel's daughter. From the quad at the high school."

"Is she okay?" I ask, pushing past him.

"She needs her rest," he says, holding his arm out to stop me from entering. But I duck under his arm and walk in anyway. "Don't go in there," he calls after me.

But why would I ever listen to the weatherman?

Mom is in the hospital bed, her head bandaged up, her face bruised and swollen. "Oh my God!" I say.

A nurse enters. "Shh, shh," she tells me. "Your mom needs quiet. Her body's sustained a trauma."

"Mommy!" I say. I haven't called her that since I was ten. Seeing her there so helpless, I start to cry again. And then outside, the rain starts. I hear it pelt against the window.

"Why don't you step into the hallway with your father," the nurse says.

"He's not my father," I tell her.

"We need her environment to be peaceful," she says.

I whisper to my mom that I love her, hoping she can hear me, hoping she understands.

When I step into the hallway, Felix is still there but not Duncan.

"I need to see Curtis really quickly," I whisper to him as we start walking.

"Chloe, I don't understand what the hell is going on."

"I don't, either."

But that's not true. I did something wrong, somehow, and these are the consequences.

"Room 427," he says, sighing. "I'll go get my car and meet you downstairs in ten. You okay?"

I nod yes, though I'm not.

I make my way up to room 427, and there, looking super small and wrapped in bandages, is Curtis Reed, another victim of my selfish, stupid act. "I'm so sorry," I say when I walk in. I'm trying not to start crying again.

"Hey, Chlo," he says, lifting his hand to wave. "Ow, ow," he says, returning it back to the bed. "*I'm* so sorry. Such an idiot. I thought I could squeeze in a quick run on Devil's Peak. What are the chances I'd arrive the same time as an avalanche? It was such a good day . . . until it wasn't."

I pull a chair up next to his bed, feeling like I'm going to faint again. The television is on, but I can't bring myself to look up. "I really don't want to, but I think I have to go home," I tell him.

He cocks his head to the side.

"I was only supposed to be gone for a few hours," I say, "and now here it is seven hours later and a hospital bill to boot. Felix is gonna take me back, but I just wanted to thank you for inviting me up. I mean, despite all this. How long are you going to have to be here?"

"I don't know yet. My parents are on their way," he says. "I have to get surgery."

"I'm so glad you're okay," I say.

"I'm actually not."

"I mean *alive*."

He looks at me like he's angry, and then like he's going to respond. But nothing comes out of his mouth.

Then I realize it's not that he's angry; it's that he's going to kiss me. And even though I can now read it—it's in his eyes—he's still not doing anything. I've certainly never done this before, though have written extensively about it in my journal.

Just kiss him, I tell myself. *You're Mother Nature. This is all part of nature—the stars kissing the sky, the sky kissing the ocean, the ocean kissing the sand.*

I recall what Grandma always said: that it's *humans* who get in the way of nature. And now here I am getting in my own way.

I close my eyes and picture our lips touching, and in my mind I see how perfectly they fit, how right they feel together. I take a chance, lean down, and plant a long, meaningful kiss on Curtis's lips. And when I do, it's exactly how I thought it would feel in all my imagining.

"Thank you," he says when I pull away. "I've been wanting to do that for a while."

"You have?"

"You have no idea," he says.

Wow. I guess not.

I stand up, but instead of leaving, I climb into his bed and boldly join him under his covers, which is no easy feat among the wires and machines to which he's attached.

"Whoa," he says, laughing, as I struggle to move in next to him. "It took a near-death experience for you to—"

But before he can finish speaking, I lean over gently and kiss him again. I think about the hearts I drew in my notebook so long ago. The fantasies in my journal. The times I could barely talk to him, or even look at him in Chorus.

"Is it the hospital gown that's turning you on?" Curtis says, laughing, putting his good arm around me.

As Journey suggested, I won't stop believing. We kiss again.

Chapter Twenty-Two

I press the button to call the elevator to take me to the lobby, and when the doors open, Duncan Sunshine is there. In one swift move, he pulls me toward him.

"Don't," I say. "Let go of me! What are you doing?"

"I know your secret," he says in a deep voice.

"Let go!"

He releases my arm, and when the doors shut, he pulls the emergency stop so the elevator can't move.

"I've got to go," I say. "My friend is waiting for me."

"You're so young," he says, his voice softening. "Don't you want to be carefree? It's your mother who deserves the powers. I know you agree."

Oh God! Did he just say what I think he did? But of course she told him. She couldn't help herself. If *she* couldn't be Mother Nature, she must have let it drop that she didn't want *me* to be.

I think about the avalanche and all the injuries, and college and Curtis. I do just want to be a kid. I do just want to be normal. But I can't jump ship.

"Chloe," he says. "I know . . ."

"She can't," I stammer. "She's all messed up," I say, pointing upward to her room. But I don't only mean because she's in the hospital. I mean messed up in so many other ways.

"Chloe. Your mom was next in line. You know that's how it works. You know how unfair it is that she was skipped over."

I feel the device in my pocket, hard and solid. I think about kissing Curtis in the hospital bed. I think about all the people who were just having a fun day on the mountain, some now in the hospital, one gone forever.

"You're not ready for this. You nearly killed your mother."

There were so many times I wanted to kill her, metaphorically speaking, and now here she is in a hospital all because of me. It's true.

"This job is mine," I tell him. "And before that it was my grandmother's, and before that her mother's . . ."

"Was your grandmother sixteen when she became Mother Nature?" he asks.

"Yes," I say. "Well, she had five years of training with her mother."

"So she was twenty-one. You're sixteen, Chloe—you're so young. Too young. Do the right thing and give the job over to your mom, where it belongs."

All I want is to be out of this stupid hospital, down the mountain, and safe in my bed at home. I don't want to deal with any of this anymore. I want to kiss Curtis, apply for colleges, read *The Tempest*, sing Journey.

"It's not easy," I say. "None of it's easy. She'd have so much to do. She'd have to read *The Book of Nature* cover to cover. That's the same book she threw in the pool, by the way."

"Listen," he says. "You're not a mother, and you don't have time for nature. Your mom's a mom, *and* she has time!"

Grandma would kill me—but I'm exhausted, and I'm trembling from low blood sugar, and I'm about to pass out from the antiseptic hospital smells, and I'm feeling claustrophobic in this elevator.

I am seriously considering his suggestion when I decide I have one more question for this weatherman. "Duncan Sunshine's not your real name, is it?"

He looks offended, but he leans in close to me and whispers, "No. It's John Buenaventura. But it's a mouthful for TV."

I appreciate his honesty.

The thought of being free of this responsibility right now suddenly makes me feel light and tingly.

"Go back up and tell your mom," he suggests. "You will make her so, so, so happy. News like that will help her recover."

"But what about her concussion?" I say.

"She'll heal!" he says. "The human body is a marvelous healer."

My mind is swirling with possibilities. *Grandma's gone*, I tell myself. *She won't know.* I can try to rewrite my life, pick up where I last left off, before I was given the powers, before I was in charge of the elements. People on this mountain, enjoying themselves one minute, and the next, buried in snow. Someone died today. Because of me. A gust of wind blows through me, and I take it as a sign.

I finally answer, "Fine," and Duncan releases the emergency stop and presses the button for my mom's floor. He lets me step out of the elevator first, but then leads me down the hallway and back into my mom's room.

She's still fast asleep, but he nudges me to speak. "It's good for her," he says. "She can hear you."

"Mom," I whisper. "I'm giving you the powers. I can't be responsible for all this anymore." I look at Duncan after I say it, and he nods in agreement. "It's your birthright," I continue. "And when you're better, I'll work with you to sort everything out."

I take the key from around my neck and carefully place it around hers. I feel for the device in my pocket. Duncan watches my hand. I don't like the way he's looking at me, so I resolve to hold on to the device a little bit longer until Mom is safely home.

I run back to the elevator and glide down to the lobby, wondering if I did the right thing.

"I don't even understand what's happening," Felix says as we're cruising down the mountain. The road is slick with rain, and I feel bad that he has to navigate it in the dark. "A minute ago you were in a hospital bed, and now we're going home?"

"I did a thing. And I don't know if it was the right thing."

"The avalanche?" Felix asks.

"I meant something else, but that was supposed to be a squall."

"What did you do?"

I contemplate how to tell him, because saying it out loud will make it true.

"I just gave up my powers. To my mom."

Felix swerves.

"Stop!" I say.

"Why would you do that?"

"It felt right?" I say. "I can't do this anymore."

"Chloe," he says in a tone that sounds like he thinks it's the worst decision I've ever made in my life.

"What-y," I retort, the way I used to as a kid when someone I didn't like called my name.

"Nothing," he says, resigned. "It's your call."

Once we're farther down the mountain and have cell reception, I phone Dad. He's shocked to hear Mom was involved in the avalanche he heard about on the news. He doesn't ask more questions. He tells me that he'll head to the hospital and watch over her.

When Felix pulls into my driveway, he says, "Pinky-swear you'll never, ever drag me up a mountain again."

"I full-body swear," I promise, leaning over to hug him.

"Question, though," he says. "What happened in that hospital room with Curtis? You're smiling too wide, all things considered."

I can feel myself blushing before I even get the words out.

And when I do, Felix blushes, too.

I call the hospital to check in on Mom every hour, and at eight o'clock, Dad says he's there, and she's awake and answering questions.

"Honey," Mom says when he hands her the phone.

"You're okay!" I say.

"I didn't know what was going on," she says. "I woke up and saw Daddy."

Uh-oh, I think. *Something's really wrong. She's never referred to him as Daddy before.*

"And for a split second," she says, "I went back sixteen years in my mind and thought I was giving birth to you!"

Okay, weird.

I'm waiting for her to drag me for the avalanche, or at least to ask me about the key around her neck. But she doesn't. She says, "I'm so grateful to be alive. I've never felt so grateful."

I hear my dad in the background say, "Laurel," in a really kind tone.

"Daddy's going to drive me home tomorrow," she says. "I have to stay over one more night."

"Okay," I say, wondering where Duncan went.

"You okay alone at home?"

"Yeah," I say. In the quiet, I'll be able to attack the piles of homework on my desk. My Chemistry assignment, the Shakespeare play I need to finish—or rather, start—and all the papers I need to write.

"I'm holding the key in my hand, honey," she says. "You made the right decision."

"There's so much to tell you," I say. "To teach you."

"I know. And when I'm back, we'll start. I promise, you can trust me."

It's like her concussion softened her or something, or maybe it was finally getting the powers.

When we hang up, I realize I still don't know if she said yes to Duncan's proposal. I wonder if he even got the chance to ask.

Next, I dial Curtis's cell phone, and before it even rings, someone picks up but doesn't speak.

"Hello?" I say cautiously into the silence.

"Oh, hello," someone says—a woman, maybe his mother.

"Hi. Is Curtis there, please?"

The woman's voice perks up. "Is this Brooklyn, sweetie?"

"No," I say forcefully. "It's Chloe. Chloe Lovejoy."

"Hello," she says, less enthusiastically. "This is Nancy, Curtis's mom. I'm afraid he's . . . occupied at the moment." And the way she says it leads me to believe it's code for *He's in the bathroom*. "I'm not sure if you know, but Curtis was in an accident. He was injured in the avalanche in Mount Kismo."

"Yes," I say. "I know. I was there with him!"

"You what?"

"I was there, too. I was calling to see how the surgery went," I explain.

"Tell me your name?" she says.

"Chloe," I say again, finding myself hopeful that maybe she's heard of me somehow. I mean, not the crawling under the covers part, but . . . something.

"Ah," she says. "I'll let him tell you about surgery when he's up for talking. He has your number, Lori?"

"It's *Chloe*."

"All right," she says, not repeating my name. "I'll let him know." And she hangs up without even saying goodbye.

* * *

The sky is inky black, and blackbirds keep circling outside my bedroom window. I try to ignore them, but they're cawing so loud I'm forced to listen. I remind myself to trust Mom. She's my mom! She gave birth to me. She was supposed to be Mother Nature in the first place. I keep convincing myself I've done the right thing, my thoughts circling around like the flying blackbirds.

I open *The Comedy of Errors* and attempt to write my Shakespeare paper. I never realized I could identify with Shakespeare so much until analyzing this play about twins separated at birth. Like the characters in my own non-Shakespearean family, the play revolves around false identities and family secrets. I decide that I'm going to write about the topic of identity crisis—because, boy, can I relate to that theme. I open a document on my computer and watch as the cursor blinks in anticipation of my first words.

After two hours of writing, I just can't concentrate anymore. I'm feeling jumpy and distracted, so I go downstairs into Grandma's room and turn on the TV to calm myself. There he is—Duncan—on the ten o'clock news. He's all smiles, all teeth.

"It's Duncan Sunshine! And I've got some great news for you, folks! Mother Nature shares my last name—Sunshine!—for the next few days, until this weekend, when a big storm is going to roll in from the west, bringing with it wind and hail. Trust me, viewers, you're gonna wanna tune in at eleven to find out more!"

I snap off the TV. What is he talking about? What big storm? Mom's not even home from the hospital yet; she definitely hasn't been in the Maparium. I navigate through the device, checking on things. It will be weird giving this up to Mom, too.

I miss Grandma so much as I sit here alone in her room. I stand and open her closet door, reach for her blue uniform, and take in a deep inhale. It still smells like her. I breathe her in, wondering if she'll ever forgive me.

In Chemistry on Monday, Mr. Kortege circles the classroom, slamming our midterms down on our desks. Next to me, Arsenic fist-pumps excitedly when he gets his, and I glance over and see he received a D. When Kortege gets to me, he slams down a big, fat red A. He stares at me, and I smile broadly. And then, miraculously, he breaks his stare and returns the smile. "An uptick," he says before walking away.

Normally, I wouldn't believe it—wouldn't think myself worthy of that grade. But I am proud—very proud—and can't contain myself when I say out loud so everyone can hear: "I got an A!" Arsenic claps his hands, and then, surprisingly, the rest of the class joins in.

After English, Mr. Rosenberg asks me to stay after class. I think I'm in some sort of trouble again. "Chloe, I'm so happy to see you involved in class and enjoying Shakespeare."

Phew!

"It's hilarious," I say. "When Antipholus of Syracuse says 'Your sauciness will jest upon my love, and make a common of my serious hours'—"

"We'll have to keep an eye out for any productions that might be coming through town. I'm very impressed at your improvement in my class," he says. "And I wanted to tell you to keep up the good work."

I smile. "Thank you," I say, gazing down toward my feet. I've never been complimented by a teacher before, let alone twice in one day.

"Oh, and there's one more thing," he says. "Come with me." He grabs his keys off the desk and motions for me to join him.

I follow him out the door and down the hallway, wondering for a minute if he's walking me to Mrs. Otsawa's office for some strange reason. But instead he leads me outside and to a rack of bikes parked next to the quad. "Ta-da!" he says with a flourish as he points to a dark-green bicycle on the end. "I ditched the car, like you suggested to Brooklyn the other week."

I can't believe my English teacher is trying to impress me.

"Congratulations!" I say. "Wow."

"I can't tell you how much I'm saving on gas, and Mrs. Rosenberg is very pleased with my weight loss," he says, sucking in his belly and patting it.

Ew.

"By the way, whatever this is," he says, pointing to my outfit, my flower-print leggings and sunflower T-shirt, "it's adorable. Just the color we need in these dark times."

Oh gosh, if he only knew the latest. I guess I can ditch these vintage clothes and go back to my old style, if one could call it that. I don't even know who I am anymore.

"The theme for today's Life Skills class is 'relationships,'" Ms. Hampton says. "Whatever that means to you. It could be a romantic relationship, or a relationship with a sibling, a parent, a friend, whoever. The only parameters for discussion are the ones we always follow: Speak from the heart, listen from the heart, and don't judge."

Peripherally, I can see Brooklyn glaring at me from across the circle, and I pray there's not enough time in today's class for her to get the Talking Stick. Ms. Hampton hands it to Tim, and he chooses to talk about his relationship with God, and I have to really, truly restrain myself from rolling my eyes.

I've never been a religious person. My mom bought me a kid's Bible when I was seven, and it sat on my bookshelf, unread for months, until I finally donated it to the Little Free Library in our neighborhood. I had friends, like Shannon, who went to church on Sundays with their family, but I didn't grow up that way. I've never believed in the man upstairs with the white beard, but now I'm not sure what to believe anymore.

Brooklyn does get the Talking Stick toward the end of class, and she says, "I had a relationship with someone that was flowing until someone else interrupted that flow." She points the stick in my direction and waves it around. "Someone from this class."

Everyone looks my way, but I don't meet anyone's gaze. Instead, I concentrate on the sound of blood rushing through my ears.

"Brooklyn," Ms. Hampton says. "We certainly don't name names or point fingers in—"

Brooklyn barrels right over her. "Someone in this class thinks she can muscle into my dating life and get her own date with him," she says.

"Brooklyn!" Ms. Hampton says sternly.

"It's okay," I say. "This is Life Skills, after all, and sometimes life just isn't fair. It was *one* dance in October. One night, Brooklyn. He pity-accepted your—"

"Chloe," Ms. Hampton says. "You don't have the Talking Stick."

Brooklyn tosses it across the circle, and I catch it just before it can whack me in the face. I hold it up like a flag in my right hand. "Sometimes singing together in a chorus is a bonding experience," I explain. "And a tragedy together on a ski slope is even more so."

"Yes, it is," Brooklyn yells from across the circle. "When *me* and Curtis are snowboarding together, and an avalanche strikes and we're both almost killed, it *is* a bonding experience."

Ms. Hampton looks defeated. "Brooklyn," she says weakly.

"I've got the Talking Stick," I remind her.

"Class is over," Ms. Hampton says, looking at her phone.

"We've got three more minutes," Brooklyn says, pointing to the wall clock above the door. "Where was it that you learned the 'life skill' of crawling under the hospital covers with Curtis?" she asks, and the rest of the class emits a collective gasp.

"That's it!" Ms. Hampton says, standing up. "Class is over. Brooklyn, Chloe, stay here with me. Everyone else is dismissed. And, remember, nothing leaves this room."

Our classmates practically run out the door.

Ms. Hampton says, "I did not get my master's degree in education to deal with quibbling!"

"But—" Brooklyn starts.

"No 'buts,'" Ms. Hampton says. "I have worked very hard to convince the administration at this school that Life Skills is an imperative course, and all your drama, all your tit for tats, all your petty teenage sh—stuff—is going to be the downfall of my legacy. Capisce?"

She stares intently at both of us. Then she pivots and walks out of the classroom, slamming the door behind her.

"I don't speak French," Brooklyn says to the closed door.

"That was Italian," I say.

I catch up with Felix in the hallway. "You're never gonna guess what just happened in Life Skills with Brook—"

But before I can even finish her name, let alone the sentence, he lifts his hand to silence me.

"What?" I say.

"I can't," he says.

"You can't what?"

"I can't keep hearing about her. I'm sorry, but you're becoming insufferable!"

"*I'm* insufferable?"

"Look," he says. "I know it's your thing to hate on Brooklyn, but—"

"She's such a bitch!" I snap, annoyed because it sounds like he's defending her.

"She's got *stuff*," he says. "Just the way you've got stuff, I've got stuff, everyone's weathering their own storms. From her point of view, *you've* gotten attention for your native garden, *you're* getting the guy she wanted . . . In her mind *you're* the bitch, when you really think about it."

In fact, I had never thought of it that way. Not ever.

"Now you look like you're going to cry," he says. "Chlo, I didn't mean to make you cry. I'm just Brooklyn-weary. I'm trying to be honest. You're so much more than this."

I nod. As hard as it is to hear, deep down I know he's right.

“You’re the *ocean,*” he says, “and you’re acting like . . . like . . . a stream.”

“Streams are important,” I say. “You have no idea how much animal life they support!”

“But you know what I mean,” Felix says.

I’m the ocean, and yet I gave it all away.

Chapter Twenty-Three

Mom is home from the hospital when I get back from school. She and Dad are sitting in the living room. Mom's in a yellow robe, her feet propped up on the coffee table.

"You're back!" I announce, but immediately I notice the key isn't around her neck. "Where's the—?" I run my fingers along my own neck.

"It's in the suitcase," Mom says, pointing toward the stairs. "I'll unpack soon."

"You will not," Dad says. "You've got to take it easy, Laurel, like the doctor said."

I reach for the device in my pocket. "I have to give you this, too," I say.

Dad takes it from me, and gently hands it over to Mom, who nods and looks my way.

Before I walk out of the room, I glance down at Mom's ring finger, but I don't see an engagement band. Phew!

"We have to look at *The Book of Nature* together," I remind her.

Dad lifts his hand. "When she's ready."

But it's not like that. Nature can't wait for her. She has to rise to the occasion no matter how she feels.

I don't tell her any of that. I have to trust that things will work out.

It's a sunny day, as Duncan promised on the news last night, but it's hot—too hot for December. I go to the backyard and dangle my feet in the pool while reading Shakespeare. Seeing my parents together in the living room is as foreign as the language in this play. I glance at the office, thinking about how I'd normally be in there. I don't care what Felix insinuated; it feels good to have this freedom.

When I look again, I see a crutch, and then I realize it belongs to Curtis, who is now hovering over me.

"Your parents told me to go around the back," he says. "I'm glad your mom's out of the hospital, too."

I scramble up from the pool. "Hi!" I say. "Hi!"

"A little casual reading?" he jokes, acknowledging the play.

I wave my hand dismissively. "Yeah, yeah, light poolside Shakespeare." I can't believe Curtis Reed is in my backyard. "Hi," I say again. "Are you supposed to be up and about?"

"Probably not."

"How'd you get here anyway? Tell me you didn't drive."

"Uber," he says. "I'm not even supposed to be moving around yet, but my parents are at work, so I put a pillow under my covers and snuck out. Like Ferris Bueller. Do you know that movie? That's where I got the idea. Plus, I wanted to see you."

I blush. Then I lead him over to the patio furniture and take hold of his crutches while he settles into the yellow lounge chair.

"What happened to your leg? I thought it was your collarbone."

"It was sort of head-to-toe everything," he says.

I can tell he's in pain, but when he tilts his head up toward the sun I sense him relax a little.

"Can I ask you something?" I venture. "Brooklyn . . . How did you even meet her?"

"She was in my Life Skills class last year."

"Wait, but how's that possible? She's in my Life Skills class now." And then I have an inkling of a realization. "Did she not pass Life Skills last year?"

"It's entirely possible," he says. "She talked over the teacher all the time and always thought she had better suggestions."

"Brooklyn Weber failed Life Skills?" I double over in laughter. It couldn't be more perfect!

I can't tell if it's my imagination, but the birds are chirping extra-loud right now. I'm trying to control my smile.

"Who would have thought that a routine trip up to Kismo would turn out to be so transformative," Curtis says. "In *so* many ways."

A few squirrels descend from the trees behind the office and stare at us before scurrying away.

"Do you promise when I'm all healed up, you'll come back up and we can finish that snowboard lesson?"

"Oh, I don't know about that," I say.

He looks down at his lap and shrugs.

"But I hope we can hang out more at maybe lower elevations," I suggest.

"Like here in your backyard."

"Totally."

Suddenly, three ducks fly in and land on the grass before waddling their way toward the pool. Curtis tries to turn, but he stops and winces.

"Oh, you okay?" I ask.

"I was going to kiss you," he says, "but I'm kind of broken."

"I'm not," I say, and scooch my chair closer to his. I move his crutches out of the way. I'm about to lean my head on his shoulder but he says, "No, no, no, it's still so painful. Sorry."

"Are you going to be able to sing at the solstice concert?" I ask.

"I didn't break my vocal cords!" he says. "I guess I'll have to sit or something."

I take his good hand, the one not hanging in a sling, and together we quietly watch the ducks swim around in the pool, me silently wondering why they're still following me since I gave up my position.

"Hey," Curtis says. "Do you want to practice?"

I nod, and he fishes for his cell phone, navigates to a musical version of one of our Christmas songs, and we belt it out, harmonies and all.

Chapter Twenty-Four

When I dress for school the next day, I don't put on any of my flowy, flowery clothes. Instead, I grab a black T-shirt and jeans, and instead of biking, I leave a little earlier than usual and walk to campus.

I can't even bring myself to look at the gardens in front of the houses as I pass. I put one foot in front of the other and concentrate on the concrete sidewalk. I don't want to see birds and bees and flowers. None of it's my responsibility anymore. I'm hoping

Mom is well enough for me to start teaching her things when I get home.

Suddenly, a horn beeps, and when I look up I see Shannon in her green Jeep. "What are you doing?" she calls out the window. "Hitchhiking?"

She pulls over, and I'm so happy to climb into her front seat—just like old times. I slam the door shut once I'm in, but she doesn't start driving.

"What?" I say.

"What do you mean, 'What'?" she says.

"A lot's happened in the past few days."

"Uh . . . yeah," she says. "Where do you wanna start?"

"Probably Curtis," I say sheepishly.

"Really?" she says. "Not the avalanche in Kismo?"

"It was supposed to be a squall. I screwed up somehow."

"All those poor people," Shannon says.

"Someone died," I say, covering my face with my hands. "I can't do it anymore. I'm done with Mother Nature. I gave it to my mom. I gave it up. I gave up."

"But Chlo—the tree . . . in the quad. That was amazing."

"I know. It was so cool. But I just wanna be . . . normal, y'know? Like you."

"Oh my God, I love that you think I'm normal," she says. "Well, Felix told me everything. And by everything, I mean *everything*. And look at you! Kissing Curtis in a hospital bed? And this may sound weird, but I'm super proud of you. I mean, a few months ago you were eating a Curtis cupcake, and now . . ."

"And now I almost killed him."

"But you didn't."

"He's the best kisser," I say, and we both shriek with joy. "When they said junior year was going to be wild, I didn't think *this* wild."

Shannon says, "How could you ever have imagined?"

I enter English class ready for Shakespeare, but it suddenly feels hot—sticky, sickly hot. I take off my sweater.

In the middle of class, I raise my hand.

"Chloe?" Mr. Rosenberg says.

"Is it true that some people believe Shakespeare didn't write all his plays?" I ask.

"Ha," he says. "Where did you hear that?"

"I read it while I was doing research for my paper."

He nods and walks to the front of the class. "It's a loaded question, Chloe. But a good one."

I smile, proud to be called out for asking a good question.

"There are many theories on the subject," he says. "Some say he wasn't educated enough for such complex thoughts and words. Others suggest his friend Christopher Marlowe was the true author of the works. And still others think women were behind these great works, citing all the strong female characters.

"But what do you think? I'll turn this question back to you. Do you think it's possible for one person to create the depth and breadth of work that Shakespeare did?"

My thoughts go immediately to Grandma. One person creating perfectly sunny days, mudslides, and hurricanes, swiping rainbows, starting forest fires. One person trying to maintain balance and harmony all across the world. Grandma and her mom, and her mom.

"Yes," I say. "I believe one person can do something that big. But it must have been a shit ton of work."

When I get home, I call out for my mother, but she doesn't answer. I go to the Maparium and try the door, but it's locked. I knock. "Mom?" I call. "Are you in there?"

It's dead silent. I don't think she is.

Upstairs, I peek into her room and see she's fast asleep on her bed. Her room is so stuffy. Every day feels like it's slowly getting hotter, and I have this weird feeling like I'm a lobster in a pot of boiling water. I look around for the device, but I don't see it anywhere.

Downstairs, I switch on the Weather Channel. The anchor, a woman, looks concerned. "All around the world, we are receiving reports of shocking and dangerous natural phenomena. In Bristol, England, a giant sinkhole opened up, causing widespread damage in the neighboring communities; the city of Naples has been evacuated over fears that legendary volcano Mount Vesuvius might erupt for the first time since 1944; and we are just getting word of a blizzard in Maui."

I click to our local news. "Let's go to our meteorologist Duncan Sunshine, out in the elements. Duncan?"

"Thanks, Holly," he says, smiling wide. "I'm out here in the middle of a scorching heat wave that I'm certain will break in the next few days. Remember I told you that when it does. And I called the blizzard in Hawaii the other day, remember? I'll admit the sinkhole in Bristol was a surprise, but I'm Duncan Sunshine, batting a thousand—or at least nine hundred."

The world is falling apart, I think. I feel like crying.

Felix calls. "Listen. Can you do anything about this heat?" he whispers. "I'm melting."

"I know. It keeps getting hotter. I don't know what's going on," I whisper back. "My mom's sleeping again, and I can't get into the office. When she wakes up, I'll show her how to cool everything down."

"Shannon's over," Felix says. "Her air-conditioning broke."

"Chlo," she says in the background. "This is bad."

"Very bad," I say, getting more nervous.

Mom's bedroom door is closed and locked when I head back upstairs. I knock hard and eventually hear a muffled "What?" from the other side.

"I can't get in, Mom."

When she finally lets me in, she's wearing pj's and bunny slippers.

"Mother," I say, "we've got to go into the Maparium."

She turns around and climbs back into bed.

"Mom!"

"I don't feel well," she says, pulling the covers over her head. "And I don't think looking at screens is going to be good for my concussion."

I kneel down on her side of the bed, like she's the kid and I'm the adult. "But, Mom, we've got to deal with this. Things aren't right. It's too hot. Strange things are happening everywhere."

She burrows in deeper.

"Fine," I say. "Where's the key? I'll go."

But she doesn't move.

"Mom! I need the key!"

I glance around the room. I try to ignore the bottle of wine on her nightstand. I don't even see a glass, just a bottle. She's doing *that* now?

"I don't know where the key is. Duncan was here visiting yesterday, and I fell asleep. When I woke up it was gone."

"What?"

"He's a meteorologist. It's okay."

I feel myself deflate like an old balloon.

"He's a *weatherman*!" I remind her. "He's basically a failed actor who talks about the weather on TV."

"Please don't yell," she says. "I have a headache."

"Where's the device?" I ask, my hand reaching out.

But she looks sheepish. "I think he took that, too."

I should have known it was a mistake when he convinced me to give up my powers. He got me when I was stressed and exhausted, and I fell right into his trap.

Slowly, like a bear emerging from hibernation, Mom comes out from under the blankets. The static makes her hair stick up.

"Mom," I say. "It's *Mother* Nature, not *Father* Nature. And he's not part of the Lovejoy family anyway. You have to fix this. You have to get the key back." But even as I say it, my words fizzle to the floor. How can I expect her to fix this when she can't even fix herself?

On my way out of her room, I throw open the windows to try and get a breeze, but the only thing that circulates is hot air.

I want to reach out to Wade, but I can't get in the Maparium. And, worse, he doesn't even know I handed all this over to Mom. I knew I should have told him, but I just couldn't bring myself to do it.

What can *I possibly do?* I ask myself.

I look up the address of our local TV station, and though it's on the other side of town, and a bit late for a field trip, I grab my bike, my helmet, and a headlamp, and pedal like mad through the dark streets.

I know Duncan Sunshine must be at the station, since there's always a weather segment on the late news. I think of things to say to him the whole ride over—insults and threats—but I realize that's not going to help me get the key back, or the device. I'm going to have to play nice.

I lock my bike outside the news building. There's a security guard just inside. He stands when he sees me.

"Hello there," he says.

"Hi," I say. "I need to see Duncan Sunshine."

The guard comes closer. "Young lady," he says. "Isn't it a little late? Shouldn't you be in bed?"

"It's urgent. I need to talk to him."

"Where are your parents?" he asks skeptically.

"I don't need my parents' permission to be here!" I say, trying to remain calm.

"Ah," he says. "Another 'nature warrior'! Why don't you write down your name and address, and we'll get a signed headshot sent to you."

"No, no," I start. "I'm not a fan. I know him, and need to speak with him. It's private, and it's important."

But the guard is having none of it, not even when I start to explain that Duncan Sunshine is dating my mother. I can hardly believe it when he puts his fingers in his ears and says, "La la la la . . ."

"Can I at least leave him a note?" I ask.

And with that, he walks to his desk, grabs a pen, and rips a piece of paper from a thick notepad.

This is Chloe, I scribble. *Return the key and the device immediately.* Then I add, *No questions asked*—like I've seen on TV in those police shows.

Oh, I have questions. But I'll sacrifice them if it means getting everything back.

The ride home is longer and harder than the ride there, and mostly uphill. I hear the faint sound of ocean waves, but there are no woodland creatures following me, no birds above. It's a long, lonely trek back to my house that hardly feels like a home these days.

I toss and turn all night. I don't know what to do. Everything's swirling in my head, and I can't calm it down enough to think straight. It's so hot out I can't even find a cool spot on my very own sheets. What could Duncan possibly be up to with this heat wave? With sinkholes in England and blizzards in Hawaii? He has no idea how to use the device. He's messing everything up and causing chaos.

I bring a bag of ice into bed with me, but it melts immediately, and now I'm sharing my bed with a bag of water. I kick the sheets off, wondering if Duncan has the brainpower to figure out how to end this heat.

Suddenly, I'm sitting on a rock in a garden. Or is it the park? And there are butterflies surrounding me, and they're so colorful and pretty. But when they land on the rock, they instantly melt. I keep trying to stop them from landing. I keep trying to catch them in the air. Then, farther away, on the swings, a kid is swinging. I call for her to help me. When I look closer, it's Grandma. But not old Grandma; it's young Grandma—maybe my age—with a big smile across her face.

"You let them go!" she says about the butterflies.

"No," I explain. "I have to catch them to save them from melting."

"You let them go," she says again.

Now, butterflies are falling from the sky and evaporating when they land, and even before they land, and Grandma morphs into Duncan Sunshine, and his teeth are gleaming and catching the sunlight and burning the butterflies in midair. When he opens his mouth to speak, it's Grandma's voice that comes out. "I just didn't know that I couldn't trust you," she says.

"But you can," I plead. "Of course you can. I'm your granddaughter! It's *Mom* you can't trust!"

The butterflies are melting by the dozens, then by the hundreds, and then by the thousands.

"I'll fix it!" I scream. "It won't be this way ever again!"

When I wake, I worry I've peed in my bed. But it's just that I've rolled over the bag of melted ice, and it popped under my weight, spilling water everywhere.

Apparently, my note did nothing, because Duncan doesn't return the key or the device, but everyone's talking about the heat wave at school the next day, and I've never felt so helpless in my life. People aren't even eating outside in the quad, because it's too hot.

I walk the other way when I see Brooklyn in the distance, but she's carrying a bullhorn, so it's hard to ignore her.

“Rally against climate change,” she calls. “Winter solstice. Rally against climate change, Morro Rock, winter solstice. If you think this is bad, just wait—it’s gonna get worse!”

I hear her loud and clear, and, for the first time ever, I agree with her.

Chapter Twenty-Five

On the afternoon of the solstice concert, I peek through the curtains of the auditorium and see Dad in the audience. I can't remember the last time he came to any of my extracurricular activities, not that there have been many. Normally, Grandma would be here, perched in the front row, a big smile across her face. Dad's toward the back, with an old-school video camera around his neck. How embarrassing.

"Oh God," I say.

"Stage fright?" Curtis says, hobbling over to me.

"No, Dad fright," I say, pointing.

"Tell me about it," he says. "My whole family is here, too, on the side. Are they gonna follow me to college?"

We both laugh nervously.

"My mom's still recovering," I say, explaining her absence.

When the lights dim, Mrs. Otsawa comes up to the stage to introduce us. Then the curtains part, and the whole Chorus class is in position, all of us standing except Curtis, who's sitting on a chair in the front row.

"Try to put your mind in winter," Mrs. Otsawa tells the audience, "as hard as that might be right now during this heat."

Ms. Cassidy enters to applause and takes her seat behind the piano. We begin with "Silent Night" and "Winter Wonderland."

Ms. Cassidy then announces that our next number knows no season. When she plays the first few notes of "Don't Stop Believin'," my dad fist-pumps and yells out "Yes!" and everyone in the auditorium laughs except me.

We start singing about the small-town girl.

I sing my heart out. I really feel it. And when we harmonize, I get tingles up and down my arms. It feels so good to be performing this song with my classmates. Curtis and I catch each other's eye during the chorus when he turns around, and I never want this day to end.

Our closing number is "Let There Be Peace on Earth." It starts with a single voice and builds until the entire group is singing. But in the middle of the song, the windows begin to rattle and creak. Then there's violent shaking. I look to my left and then to my right. The piano stops, and murmurs erupt from the audience. When I finally realize what's happening, I can't help yelling at the top of my lungs, "*Duncan!*" My voice echoes in the auditorium.

Everyone's looking around, gauging the situation. Some are crouching on the floor. Ms. Cassidy comes rushing over to me. "It's okay," she says, taking my arm. "It's okay. It's just an earthquake." But I muscle my way out of her grasp and bolt from the stage.

All eyes are staring as I scramble outside and hop on my bike. I can't feel my legs, and my feet keep slipping off the pedals. When I regain sensation, I feel like I'm biking through honey, all the way home.

Mom's in bed, watching news coverage of the earthquake, when I run upstairs.

"What are you doing?" she asks, "Why aren't you at the concert?"

"Where is he?" I demand. "This can't go on like this."

"It was a 6.3," she says. "Scared the crap out of me. I tried to duck and cover, but I could barely walk."

"Where is he?" I yell. "We need everything back!"

"Chloe, I don't know. He broke up with me last night. I don't know where he is."

I can't believe what I'm hearing. "He broke up with you?"

There's an aftershock, and I fall against the wall. The bottle of wine on Mom's nightstand is teetering.

"If I could turn back time, believe me, I'd do it all differently," Mom says. "I wouldn't be so scared of my own damn mother, first of all. I wouldn't believe everything she said was an objective truth. More like *her* truth."

"What is he doing?" I look back at the wine bottle. "And what are *you* doing?"

Too angry to hold back anymore, I grab the wine bottle and pour what little contents are left over her nightstand.

"Don't," she says. "Stop it. You're ruining the wood."

"You're worried about the wood?"

I smash the bottle against the wall. The glass shatters all over the place. "I don't need this," I wail.

There is fear in my mom's eyes, and I have this sudden, alarming vision of her as a little girl, no more than five, watching as her own mom stormed through life. And then I picture Mom in college, pregnant with me, having no idea that this turn of events would cause her to lose her birthright as Mother Nature herself. And I'm sure one sip of wine became three, which became thirty, and her drinking masked years of hurt and disappointment, until it started hurting me and everyone else in her orbit.

"You need help," I cry.

"*I* need help?" she says, looking around at shards of glass scattered in slivers over the floor.

"You need to go to an AA meeting. For me. For our family. But mostly for you."

"How do you know about AA?" she asks sincerely.

"I Googled 'Help drunk mother' the other night when I couldn't sleep," I say, and her face softens for a brief moment.

"I'm so sorry, Chloe." She puts her head in her hands and covers her face.

"I need to find Duncan," I say.

"I'll come with," she says, kicking the sheets off.

"You said you can't walk. I'll do it myself. Like I do everything myself."

"I can hobble," she says.

"No," I say. "You'll hold me back."

I pedal my bike in the direction of Morro Rock. During our training, Grandma said Great-Great-Great-, and maybe even three more *Greats*, Grandma had created the rock by mistake during her transition. She meant to create a volcano, but instead she made a volcanic plug. And that's why our family has stayed here, anchored by this giant hovering rock in this small California town.

The sun is hitting the rock in a way that makes it look like a massive golden nugget. It's December 21, the shortest day of the year, so why does it feel like the longest?

I see Brooklyn, leading the climate change rally she's been blabbing about. I find a place to lock my bike and fall in step with the other nature warriors.

Despite the earthquake and the melting, sticky heat that just won't quit, the rally is large and Brooklyn is in her full glory, espousing facts through a megaphone: "Melting icebergs, dying seals, drought—these are just some of the real effects of climate change. And we won't put up with it, will we?"

The marching crowd chants, "No!"

"Change has to start with us, doesn't it?" Her voice echoes through the megaphone.

"Yes!"

I can't hate her for this part of her personality, as contradictory as it is to the rest of her life. I know she planned the rally to get into college, but at least she's doing it. At least she didn't give up. The way I did.

I walk quickly along the path that leads to the rock, and what do I come upon but the local news van—and Duncan Sunshine with his cheesy smile and his stupid microphone. I've found him.

As I get close, he approaches Brooklyn. "We're coming to you live from Morro Rock," he says to the camera, "where high school junior Brooklyn Weber is holding a climate change rally."

"Hi, Duncan Sunshine," she says. "I'm so pleased you could find time in your busy schedule to cover this. Native gardens are great and all, but real change comes from loud activism, and that's what we're doing here today."

I see the outline of Grandma's key tucked into Duncan's crisp white shirt. I need it back, and I need it now.

"Right, Brooklyn," he says. "Gardens *are* great, but there is a different kind of power I'm interested in. Like the power of wind," he says. He puts his hand in his pocket—*The device! My device!*—and a strong gust of wind blows in from seemingly nowhere.

"Whoa," Brooklyn says as signs are blown out of the hands of some people in the crowd. "How'd you know that was coming?"

"I'm a meteorologist," he says. "I know things. Like I know it's going to rain so much in a few minutes that the town will flood."

"What? That's terrible," Brooklyn says.

I agree. Duncan is abusing his powers. *My* powers. For what? For fun? For fame?

"Is it terrible?" he says. "Or is it just . . . nature?"

I get the courage to stand up to him. "It's terrible," I announce on live TV. "*You're* terrible. Give me the key back."

I reach my hand out, but suddenly he drops the microphone and bolts to the base of the rock, crowded with giant saguaros. He leaps over the shorter ones, and then he starts climbing.

The rock's not meant for climbing; it's not safe. Plus, only tribal members are allowed up twice a year for ceremonies. But his fingers are deep in the crevices as he hoists himself up.

"This is man versus nature!" he calls down to people below him—and to me. The demonstrators scatter to get a better view, and others join when they hear the commotion.

"What are you doing?" Brooklyn calls through her bullhorn.

But he doesn't answer; he just keeps on climbing, his feet finding footholds on the jagged ridges.

"Something's wrong with the weatherman," she calls out. "Can someone help?"

Above the rock, deep-black clouds are rolling in, and the wind has picked up significantly. The cameraman is still rolling, and in my peripheral vision, I see police approaching. I need to do something, but what?

I can't climb that thing. It's illegal. Plus, I'm scared of heights.

I hear someone calling "Chloe!" and Felix and Shannon emerge from the crowd.

"What on earth?" Felix says, breathless.

Shannon asks, "Is the weatherman having a nervous breakdown on live TV?"

I want to tell them both that I'm about to have a nervous breakdown of my own, when the clouds open up and water starts pouring down. It doesn't feel like rain. It feels like the spout of a bathtub when turned on full-force. Boats in the harbor are pitching up and down on a sudden surge of waves, children are crying, and people are fleeing the shocking scene. It's too much.

"What is that psycho doing?" Felix asks.

"Chloe," Shannon says, "you've got to stop him!"

Duncan's almost to the top of Morro Rock, yelling to be heard. "Thunder and lightning!" he calls, and almost instantly there's a clap of thunder so loud it shakes the ground. Lightning slices the dark sky, and more people scatter from the thinning crowd.

I run over to Brooklyn, who's still standing at the base of the rock but now drenched and confused. "Hi," I say. "I need your megaphone.

"Please," I add, to be a good citizen.

Without question, she hands it to me, so I also say, "Thank you."

I hold it up to my mouth. "Get down, Duncan!" I call. "Stop it. You're causing chaos."

I'm not sure he can hear me, but he's standing on the top of Morro Rock, arms and legs outstretched. With any luck, the lightning will strike him. A boat in the harbor is cracking apart. Water is spilling onto the sidewalks and paths.

When I was little, Grandma took me to see *Fantasia*, not because she thought I'd like it, but because *she* liked it so much. It was her favorite movie from childhood. Duncan is acting like Mickey Mouse as the sorcerer's apprentice, only he's conducting controlled chaos from the top of Morro Rock. And Duncan is evil. It's not cute or fun or funny or colorful. There's no dramatic musical soundtrack behind him, only the sound of people screaming below.

"You can't do this!" I call.

I think I hear Shannon shout "A twister!" and when I turn around, I see a car in midair, spinning in the wind.

"Chloe!"

I look around to figure out who's calling my name.

"Chloe!"

I don't see anybody. But then I notice my mom wobbling toward the rock.

"No!" I beg. "Go back home!"

Mom shakes her head no.

"It's too unsafe here," I plead.

But Mom catches up to me, and grabs the bullhorn out of my hands. "Shame on you, Duncan Sunshine," she yells. "How dare you manipulate me and my daughter, only to hijack her abilities for your own selfish use."

Everything is so out of control. Someone is going to get hurt, or killed. All for what? All for nothing. No one is doing anything about him, not even the police, who are just tilting their heads up to watch.

"Be right back," I say, and I break away from everyone. What else can I do but start climbing?

I hear Felix and Shannon yelling at me to come back, but I've been pushed to my limit.

When I was thirteen, we had to climb ropes in gym class. My hands scraped against the nylon material as I lugged myself up, and when I got to the top, I let go, because I couldn't take the pain anymore. Surprisingly, I landed safely on my feet, and my friends let out a collective "Whoa." You were supposed to climb yourself down, of course, not jump like I had. But I'd made it to the top that time, and I'm determined to make it to the top again now. The rock is slippery and the wind is forceful and I'm trying not to think of how high up I am, but I find the inner strength to keep on going.

"Go, Chloe!" Is that Brooklyn over the megaphone? I think it might be, though I can't bear to look down. She starts the crowd chanting. "Go, Chlo, go, Chlo."

Hearing that gives me a boost of energy. I keep telling myself I'm an ocean, not a stream—just like Felix and I talked about.

When I finally make it to the top, Duncan looks like a wild animal conducting a weather symphony. Crows, hawks, and pelicans circle him.

"Stop!" I call over all the noise. "You've got to stop this. Why are you doing this? I need the key back!"

Duncan hears me. I know he does, because he reaches under his shirt, yanks the chain, and holds the key in his hand. Then he tosses it into the ocean below in one horrifying motion. I watch as Grandma's centuries-old key sails down the incline and into the churning sea.

"No!" I cry. "You can't do that."

"I just did," he howls.

"You're out of control!" I shout.

"I'm in perfect control," he says. "Don't you see?"

And then I stumble as I hear what sounds like Grandma's voice—like she's right next to me speaking into my ear, even though Duncan and I are the only two people up here. Is it in my head? Or is it really Grandma?

"This job is about balance and harmony, dear."

"Grandma?"

"Balance and harmony," the calm voice says again.

But what does she mean? Or rather, what does that voice mean? And where is it coming from? And how can I achieve any of that from way up here?

"When nature suffers, we all suffer, Chloe," the voice says.

It's got to be in my own head. Dead people don't talk to you. Maybe through a Ouija board, but not in person on top of a volcanic plug.

"I . . . I know," I stammer.

Above me, the birds gather, and glide together through the choppy atmosphere.

And then I hear my mom's voice from down below, through the megaphone. "How do you need me to help you? Chloe? What can I do?"

"Just keep talking to me," I yell into the air, pretty certain she can't hear a word I'm saying.

"Take one step at a time," Mom shouts. "Maybe try to stop the wind, so we can hear each other better."

The wind, the wind. I don't have the device, so I try to remember the chant. "Nolite ventus," I call. And then I say it even louder. "Nolite ventus!" The wind slows and then stops. I'm so relieved it worked that I get a little charge of excitement.

"The clouds!" Mom yells. "No more rain clouds, just the puffy kind!"

"Ultra nubes pluviam!" I say. And the gray dissolves to white.

"The ocean!" Mom yells. "Try to calm it down!"

What is the chant for the ocean? Is it "Magnum fluctus"? Something with the word *oceanum*? I can't remember. I close my eyes and try to picture a calm sea. I concentrate hard. I allow myself to look down the side of the rock. The crowd has mostly dispersed because the water is so intense. I see Mom and Shannon and Felix. I think I still see Brooklyn and a few of her nature warriors, including Hailey.

"I don't know how to do the ocean!" I call, but not loud enough for anyone to actually hear. Anyone except Duncan.

"You can't," he growls. "You are powerless now, remember?"

"I'm not! Didn't you see me quiet the wind?" I yell. "Why are you doing this?"

"You ask too many questions," he roars.

So I ask again, "Why are you doing this?"

Duncan takes a step closer. "You have no idea about corporations or media conglomerates or viewership," he says. "I went into this because I love science. I also love telling people what they can or can't expect. If someone brings an umbrella because of me? I consider it a community service.

"We have a 5.2 percent share in the market, and things have been sliding. Viewership is down 29 percent. And with AI at our heels, my job is in jeopardy. Do you know what that means? The only way to get viewers to keep tuning in is for a segment to be clickable, shareable, or to go viral! Don't you understand? There's a saying in the news biz: 'If it bleeds, it leads'—or in this case, if it floods.

"We need the viewers. The viewers need us . . . And I'm going to keep doing the weather. Throw in a wild wind advisory or heat-wave hysteria, and my viewers will never look away again. I'll get to do my job in perpetuity!"

I really have no idea what he's talking about. "You can't just play like this! A twister? Floods? Everything relies on everything else. It's called 'symbiosis.'"

"What are you talking about? Your grandmother did whatever she wanted."

"Not for *fun*," I say. "She did it because the earth required it. The land needed to regenerate or pressure needed to be released.

"Go back to being a weatherman," I yell. "You get to be on TV. Everyone loves watching you. That's powerful. You have headshots."

"I'm a meteorologist. I'm a *scientist*."

"*I'm* Mother Nature!" I howl, and the chant to quiet the ocean pops into my head. "Tranquillitas oceanum," I shout. "Tranquillitas oceanum!"

Below, the waves settle, and the bobbing boats stabilize. With the weather calmer now, from on top of the rock, I can see Morro Bay and my entire town. I think about my ancestors who saw a similar view so long ago.

I start to hear the familiar sounds of happy birds, and I see that some are flying toward me. Then I hear the low, growling hum of a helicopter, getting closer and closer. The birds scatter as the chopper descends. A man yells, "Get in!" and he throws down a rope ladder. Oh, gosh, not another rope!

I look around and suddenly realize Duncan's not here anymore. I climb the four nylon steps, and a uniformed man hoists me into the helicopter.

"It's a wet day for a climb up the rock," he tells me.

"It's actually a volcanic plug," I explain.

Out the window, I see a flock of birds following along—not just seabirds, but bluebirds, cardinals, and even an owl. It's a short ride to the helipad on top of the local hospital, but it's spectacular; I've never been in a helicopter before.

As soon as we land, a medic puts me on a gurney. "I'm fine," I say, but I am ignored.

"What happened to Duncan?" I ask. "Do you know where he went?"

"The weather guy?" he asks.

I nod.

"I think he—"

"Died?" I say, too loudly.

"Nah," he says. "He didn't die. Last I heard, he threw himself into the water. He was screaming about losing a key and rambling about being Mother Nature—something like that—and the old lady who used to be. That guy's obsessed with the weather." He points to his temple. "Somethings not right up here. They're doing a water rescue now."

I'm wheeled into a quiet room in the hospital. I don't sit on the bed but, instead, on the stool where the doctor usually sits. There's blood on my fingers from grasping at the jagged rocks. I wash my hands in the sink and bandage them up with Band-Aids I find on the shelves.

Felix pops his head into the room. "Found her!" he says, and Shannon follows him in. They both sit down on the bed. "I'm speechless," Felix says. "I can barely breathe."

"I'm hungry," Shannon says, putting her arm around Felix.

"I'm saturated," I say, still in my sopping clothes.

"This was the wildest day of my life," Felix says. "Brooklyn getting the crowd all riled up chanting for you?"

"I thought you didn't want to talk about her," I say.

"She rose to the occasion," he says. "You have to admit."

I'm looking at Shannon, her arm draped around Felix, and wondering. "Are you two . . . ?"

Felix nods.

"We're testing it out," Shannon explains. "We were gonna tell you, but, um, you've been otherwise occupied."

"You're dating!"

"We're hanging out," Felix says.

Shannon removes her hand. "We're dating!" she tells him.

"You guys!" I say, and they both smile sheepishly.

I reach over to hug them just as a doctor enters. She looks from the bed to the stool. "Okay, what's going on? Who's the patient?" she asks.

"We're all good, actually," I tell her.

"Who climbed Morro Rock?"

I reluctantly raise my hand.

"And who bandaged you up? They did a terrible job."

"I did," I confess.

"Let me fix that," she says, undoing my work and swabbing my fingers with alcohol pads before reapplying fresh Band-Aids. Everything stings.

"You're lucky that's your only injury," she says. "What were you doing up there? It's really dangerous, and I'm sure you know you're not supposed to climb it."

"I know. But I handled it," I say. "I've handled worse."

I may have sounded confident, but when the three of us exit the hospital, I'm sort of shaking. Still not finished with this disaster of a day. Still overwhelmed that Shannon and Felix are together! "There's someone I have to see," I tell my friends. "Who can drive me?"

"Not it," Shannon says. "Whoever it is you're talking about."

I look at Felix.

“You can say no,” Shannon tells him.

“No,” he says, “I can’t.”

“I have to see Wade. I have to.”

He digs in his pocket and pulls out his key fob. “Okay.” He sighs. “Let’s go.”

“Babe!” Shannon says.

“We won’t be long,” Felix assures her. “I promise, babe.”

“Oh God!” I say, covering my ears. “You can’t call each other ‘babe’ in front of me!”

But Shannon ignores me. “Babe. Babe. Babe. Babe!” she says, laughing, as I climb into the front seat of his car.

Chapter Twenty-Six

"Back to the little cabin in the woods?" Felix says as we pull out of his parking spot.

"I *have* to see Wade. Do you remember how to get there, by any chance?"

"We'll figure it out," he assures me. "Though I'm not sure what to input in the GPS."

"It's not GPS-able," I remind him. "But we'll find our way. We're good like that."

As we drive out of town, I can see Morro Rock through the side mirror. In what world was I standing on top of it? In what universe was I doing battle with the local weatherman? How is this my life, quieting storms and restoring order to chaos?

"Quick question," Felix says. "Does your boyfriend know about any of this?"

I slink down in the passenger seat, thinking, *He doesn't, but he will.* "All in good time," I say.

"You didn't even flinch when I said 'boyfriend,'" Felix says.

"I'm too tired to flinch," I admit. "Speaking of 'boyfriend' . . ."

"I mean, *you* kind of brought us together, y'know. When you really think about it."

"Oh, sure, blame me!"

"We've been on the phone for hours, Chlo, trying to digest everything. Like, sometimes we've talked till two in the morning, just processing, y'know? And, I don't know, we just realized how much we liked each other. *Love*, really."

"I guess that's part of Mother Nature's job," I say.

Eventually, and miraculously, we find our way to the brook at the base of Wade's property. We park and walk to his cabin, and I pound on the front door. "It's Chloe!" I call.

I'm hoping he's home, even though he's not expecting me. Is he even allowed to go out? How does he shop for groceries?

"Chloe Lovejoy!" I clarify, just in case he knows another Chloe.

Wade opens the door, looking concerned. "Hel—"

"Please don't be mad. Please, please . . . don't hate me. I ruined everything. He convinced me to hand the powers over to my mom, and then he stole them and broke up with her and threw the key into the ocean, and—"

"Slow down," Wade says, stepping aside and letting us both inside. The three of us stand in his hallway.

"Who broke up with whom?"

"Her mom and the weatherman," Felix says. "Duncan Sunshine. He stole the key."

"Sit," Wade says, gesturing to the couch. "Start from the beginning."

I do, and the words tumble out of my mouth like an avalanche. I tell him about climbing Morro Rock, quieting the wind, calming the ocean. I confess to my weak moment in the hospital the other day, handing over my powers to Mom, and all the mess that followed.

"Sorry. Back up," Wade says. "Calming the ocean? Without the device?"

"He had it. It was in his pocket. Duncan Sunshine's. That's not really his name, by the way."

"You calmed the ocean, Chloe?" Wade says.

"I couldn't remember the chant. I just tried to picture the opposite of a tempest. But then I remembered it. I think?"

Wade seems excited, even though he's sitting still. His hands are on his knees, and he's blinking rapidly, and his mouth is hanging open.

"When you say you pictured it, you mean in your mind?"

Felix looks at me.

"Um, yeah?" I say.

"And just out of curiosity, what were you doing when the avalanche struck?"

"We were riding up the chairlift," Felix says.

"And I was screaming because I saw my mom and Duncan below," I remind him.

"You were hella upset," Felix says.

Wade looks like he's about to lose it, but in a good way. He starts speaking really fast. "The family mythology suggests that Mother Nature's powers used to be internal, that they originated organically from emotions and intentions. But as the generations continued and technology progressed, we were able to engineer certain systems to match the earth's needs." Wade jumps out of his chair and abruptly heads toward the back of the cabin. "Come with me," he says, and Felix and I hop off the couch and fall in step behind him, practically running to keep up, toward the shed.

Wade stands me in front of one of the boards at the far end of the wall, presses some buttons, zooms in on what looks like a satellite image of Mount Kismo, and then telescopes even closer to his own neighborhood, the one where we're standing now. "Picture wind," he says excitedly. "Picture wind in your mind like you said you did with the ocean."

"Okay," I say. I squeeze my eyes shut and envision the trees around us bending and swaying, clouds moving briskly across the sky. I concentrate hard, biting my lower lip, determined to really see and feel the scene. *Wind.* I focus harder than I have for anything, ever, including my Chemistry tests, including the practice ACT, and after a few minutes I say, "I see it!" But I don't want to open my eyes. I want to stay with this image as it becomes even clearer.

"Oh my God!" Felix shouts, and I instinctively open them. There's a howling windstorm right outside the window.

"What?" I say, stepping closer to look out.

"Yes!" Wade exclaims. "You're doing it! Chloe, we haven't seen powers like these in at least six generations!"

I conjure a superbloom in Ecuador, and rainbows in New

Zealand, just by concentrating, just by visualizing, just by thinking. Then I sprout wildflowers in front of Wade's cabin. He throws his arms around me and hugs me tightly as the purple, yellow, and pink flowers spring from the ground.

"Please don't get too excited," I beg. "Please. I can't do it anymore. I'm starting to feel exhausted."

"But, Chloe—" he starts.

"She really can't," Felix chimes in. "It's stressing her out, I can tell."

Wade shifts on his feet. "Chloe, it's not something— You don't want these powers. I do understand. But the problem is, they live in you already. It's like saying you don't want your brown hair, or your blue eyes. Or your fingernails!"

Felix says, "She hates her nails. They never grow!"

"You *are* Mother Nature, Chloe. You just *are*," Wade says. "You want long fingernails? Will them to grow!"

I can't believe it's that easy, but I close my eyes and picture my fingers with long, strong nails. Felix's laughter tells me it's working, so I open one eye.

"No way!" I say. "You mean I could have done this the whole time?"

"You're a very powerful young woman," Wade says. "You'll only grow more so with age."

I let his words pour over me. I just am. There are levers and buttons and holograms on the outside, but on the inside there's my brain and my heart. My blood. My birthright. My power.

Chapter Twenty-Seven

How does it feel to find your way back to yourself? The self you didn't even know. Let me tell you: It feels fantastic.

I'm at the tailor's because I redesigned Grandma's onesie-jumpsuit into a fabulous miniskirt-overall thingy. It sounds quirky, but it looks great, and it fits perfectly. When the tailor handed it to me across the counter, he said, "Well, aren't you a ray of sunshine?" And that's it—the side of myself I never quite knew existed.

Not just the ray, but the sunshine itself.

It's kind of like when black-and-white Dorothy lands in colorful Oz, by way of a twister, might I add. Tornadoes take stuck moisture and spread it to other parts of the atmosphere. Earthquakes are needed for lakes and mountains to expand, and volcanoes erupt from built-up pressure underneath. Grandma told me all of this back on my sixteenth birthday, but I didn't hear it, couldn't understand.

I wish she could see me now, in my bright era, but something tells me she saw it even before I ever did. Practicing my inner powers with Wade was like a mirror into myself. And I rode home from his cabin with Felix a changed person.

As I walk the four blocks home from the tailor, poppies spring from the earth. Bees hum alongside me. I see Morro Rock in the distance, feel sun on my face. I smell something in the air—it's a familiar perfume, or maybe the sweet smell of hope.

At home, I duck into Grandma's room and click on the TV. A promo for the news comes on. War, political strife, tech meltdowns . . . "And closer to home," the anchor says, "an update on our very own Duncan Sunshine, who's officially taking an extended leave of absence as he recovers from his . . . inner turbulence. Stay tuned for the news at six."

When the doorbell rings, I let Curtis in, leading him back to Grandma's room, where we both sit on her bed. "There's something I need to tell you," I start, echoing the words my grandmother said to me. "There's something you need to know."

And I tell him everything. All of it. If he is going to be my boyfriend, he is going to have to know every single thing about me. No more secrets. The good, the bad, and the unbelievable.

There's a concerned expression on his face at first as he listens to me ramble. I tell him if it's too much I'll understand, but he shakes his head no.

I take him back to the office and unlock the door with the new code, and his eyebrows lift as he sees all the equipment and *The Book of Nature* for the first time. Outside, I make the lemon tree bloom in front of his eyes.

Finally, he speaks. "This feels really epic," he says.

And what can I do but agree?

"Chloe!" Mom calls from the office the next day. I hear her from the kitchen, where I'm making a quick snack, and I go to find her.

"Chloe, what does this mean again? Here, this blue dot over Norway."

"Oh, just trace it over here, like that, and, yeah, it's fine. See? There's a blue thing on the other side of the world in Antarctica."

"Ah," she says.

"If they turn red at any time, then you know a tsunami or earthquake is coming, and you just have to adjust."

Since Wade was able to install the electronic locks, I don't have to worry about Duncan ever breaking in, on the off chance he finds the key in the ocean. We never got the device back from him, either, but Wade wiped it remotely and then restored everything on a new device, adding security measures that are a pain to navigate but worth the struggle.

"Okay," Mom says. "I'm good."

"Curtis is picking me up," I say.

"Very nice boy," she says. "You have good taste."

"We're going to see the sunset."

"I'll make sure it's a good one." She winks.

"Do you want to work on new sea life later tonight?" I ask.

"Yes! I have some ideas," she says.

"Great."

She's always been the artist in the family, so I'm open to seeing what she comes up with.

"Just text if you have any questions," I remind her.

"I will," she promises. I kiss her on the cheek before dashing outside to the beautiful day.

I've decided to share the job with Mom, after clearing it with Wade. She can focus on everything inside while I'm at school, and I'll take the evening and weekend shifts, and fill in when she's at her AA meetings, which she started last week.

Both of us will figure it out one day at a time.

I have this tradition. On the first day of every new year, I choose a word to define the next twelve months. I always pick it first thing on January 1. We're now technically eight hours into the new year, and I haven't found my word yet. So I grab my phone and earbuds, put my music on shuffle, and head out for a walk, hoping the word will come to me. Hoping nature will inspire me.

"I'll be back!" I call to Mom, but I think she's in the Maparium again, because she doesn't answer.

I make a left out of our driveway and amble down the sidewalk, Frank Sinatra playing in my ears. The bird chirps are louder than the music. I smile as I cross the street toward the park. Squirrels and raccoons are following in my footsteps, and then a few cats join the parade. "That's life!" I sing along with Frank.

The salt air smells heavy but feels light and crisp. I can see Morro Rock from my vantage point. I picture myself, just the other week, on top of that rock, duking it out with the weatherman. That couldn't have been me, could it have? Me? Chloe Tara Lovejoy?

And yet it was! It so was.

I still don't have my word. *Brave* feels vague. *Strong* is meh. I can do better. I want the word to inspire my entire year, to be something I can lean into when I need it. I take a left, away from the rock, past the boulevard, headed in the direction of the nature reserve.

As I continue south, I pass the low-growing manzanita twisted along the path, the red branches vibrant against the pale sand. Grandma used to point out the California poppies, their splashy orange color distinguishing them from other flowers. It's too early for them now—they'll bloom in the next month or two—but my memories of my time with Grandma aren't restricted by season. I think about her a lot, and mostly about the little things: Watching her favorite soap opera with her, cuddled on her bed. Going trick-or-treating in the neighborhood. Eating breakfast together every day since I was a little girl.

I smile, feeling the peace of this place, my home, settling over me. The poppies will emerge, along with a host of other colorful plants and flowers, each reminding me how grateful I am to be overseeing the quiet rhythms of the wild.

Suddenly, the song comes on my mix—*our* song, mine and

Curtis's, "Don't Stop Believin'," our favorite one from the Solstice Sing Along. And as soon as I hear the opening notes, I know my word. It embodies everything that is and is going to be.

I decide right there that my word for the year is *journey*.

Because that's what I'm on. That's what we're all on. Even the butterflies. Even Duncan Sunshine, and Brooklyn, even the blades of grass that I'm stepping over. I beam as I keep strolling, the song on repeat, stopping only to pet the cats, possums, and raccoons, and all the beautiful animals that follow in my path.

Acknowledgments

The path to publication was long and circuitous, but with time and patience we made it!

Thanks to my friend and connector Fonda Snyder, I met Jane Hamilton at Jane Hamilton Literary, who became my fierce and fabulous agent.

Joy Peskin has been my dream editor at my dream publishing house.

I don't think I can properly articulate how thrilled I am to have found a home for this project with Farrar, Straus and Giroux.

Thanks to Hannah Miller, Allyson Floridia, Aster Hung, Carlee Maurier, and Samantha Sacks.

Thank you to Ben Strouse, Chris Tarry, and David Kreizman at Gen-Z Media for producing the podcast version of this story, then titled *Becoming Mother Nature*.

I was supported throughout the writing process by the

kindness and friendship of many. Some offered notes and insights on drafts, while others provided laughs and meals. In no particular order, thank you to my parents, Ron and Sheila, my sister Jennifer, Foundation Obras in Portugal (where the beginning chapters of this book were written), Mary Ore, David Rubenstein, Irene Turner, Sandra Marsh, Sarah Cypher, Max Brooks and Michelle Kholos Brooks, Erika Banks, Jen Kagan, Andy Ross, Jim Belcher, Liza Richardon, Liz Bliss, Wendy Glickman, Jill Taylor, Lori Sunkin, and so many others. Four-legged friends Percy, and then Bosley, kept the inspiration flowing.

And lastly, nature is suffering, and it's not because of a rogue weatherman or a teenage girl. It's because of us. Let's look inward and take responsibility for decisions that affect our planet. Here are some resources:

Clean Air Task Force: catf.us
Jane Goodall Institute: janegoodall.org
Natural Resources Defense Council (NRDC): nrdc.org
Rainforest Action Network: ran.org
TreePeople: treepeople.org
Waterkeeper Alliance: waterkeeper.org
Wildlife Conservation Society: wcs.org

Author photo © Kevin Salter

ABOUT THE AUTHOR

Melissa Clark is an author, television writer, podcast creator, and college instructor. Her novels include *Swimming Upstream, Slowly*; *Imperfect*; and *Bear Witness*. Melissa created, executive produced, and wrote multiple episodes of the award-winning animated television series *Braceface*, which starred the voices of Alicia Silverstone and Michael Cera; and has written scripts for *Rolie Polie Olie*, *Sweet Valley High*, and *Totally Spies!*, among others. Her episodic podcasts include *Becoming Mother Nature* as well as *Grandma for President*. She is cocreator of a true-crime podcast forthcoming from Audible. Melissa teaches writing courses at Otis College of Art and Design in Los Angeles.

@msmelissaclark

melissaclarkwrites.com